MR. MAGORIUM'S WONDER EMPORIUM

Magical Movie Novel

By Suzanne Weyn

Based on the motion picture written
and directed by Zach Helm

Scholastic Inc.
New York Toronto London Auckland Sydney
Mexico City New Delhi Hong Kong Buenos Aires

ISBN-13: 978-0-439-91250-1
ISBN-10: 0-439-91250-4

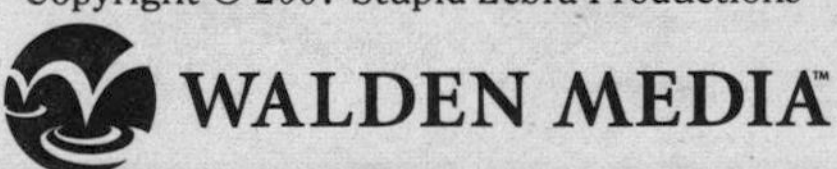

This book is published in cooperation with Walden Media, LLC. Walden Media and the Walden Media skipping stone logo are trademarks and registered trademarks of Walden Media, LLC, 294 Washington Street, Boston, Massachusetts 02108.

Published by Scholastic Inc.
SCHOLASTIC and associated logos are trademarks and/or registered trademarks of Scholastic Inc.

12 11 10 9 8 7 6 5 4 3 2 1 7 8 9 10 11 12/0

Printed in the U.S.A.
First printing, October 2007

CHAPTER ONE

Eric Applebaum had come home early from camp. Two whole weeks early, to be exact. He had begged over the phone and pleaded online with his mother. Every day he sent a postcard imploring her to come get him.

Finally she gave in. His mother agreed to bring him home on one condition — that he would try to make real, actual friends with other children over the summer. She did not want to hear about imaginary friends or animal friends or friends from books, movies, or TV. She demanded that he produce real, human, kid friends.

Mrs. Applebaum loved her son and she didn't think it

was healthy that Eric liked to play alone all the time. If he was not going to camp, she didn't want him sitting around by himself all day while she worked. And above all, she did not want him to spend all his time at that crazy toy store — Mr. Magorium's Wonder Emporium.

Eric agreed. He would try to make friends. And he meant it, truly. It wouldn't be easy, of course. He'd never had much luck making friends. He preferred playing on his own.

But he didn't promise not to go to Mr. Magorium's Wonder Emporium. He didn't say he would. But he didn't say he wouldn't, either. He sort of didn't say anything at all. The whole time he had been at camp, the only thing he had thought about was getting back to Mr. Magorium's Wonder Emporium. It was simply the most amazing place in the world. He couldn't imagine anyone ever wanting to be anywhere else. He planned to go right down to the Emporium as soon as his mother left for work the next morning.

Lots of kids came into the store. No one ever told a child to leave, and there were endless interesting toys to play with and amazing things to explore. It would be a great place for him to find other children to play with. He would just have to work up the nerve to actually talk to them.

Maybe he would start by asking someone else to play — or not. When he was around other kids, he always felt nervous and shy, afraid that they wouldn't like him. A large part of him wanted to play with the others, but a larger part found it easier to simply go off on his own.

On his first evening home from camp, Eric sat on his bed and stared into his open closet. Inside the closet was his huge collection of hats. He had collected them for years from every gift shop, catalog, and costume store he could find.

Which of his many hats should he wear the next day? It had to be just right.

Mr. Magorium would be sure to admire his hat. He always did.

After much thought, Eric picked out one of his favorites, a cowboy hat with a band made of a skin shed from a real rattlesnake.

Trying it on in front of the mirror, he smiled at his own image. Perfect. Now that camp was behind him, the rest of the summer was looking good. He would spend it playing, exploring new toys, and doing all the things he loved.

He might even make some friends.

But best of all, tomorrow he would be back at his favorite place — Mr. Magorium's Wonder Emporium.

CHAPTER TWO

Inside Mr. Magorium's Wonder Emporium, sunlight poured through the toy store's many windows. It cast a warm, orange glow. One window in particular sat above the others. It was round, stained glass, and featured a large, red M in the middle. The window scattered rainbow light across the walls and floor.

The store didn't have aisles like a regular toy store. Instead bins, barrels, baskets, and tables were placed everywhere. All of them were filled with unusual, exciting objects. Around the store were puppet theaters, play areas, and spaces to try out toys. There was a science

laboratory for experiments, a huge ant metropolis, a case containing dolls from around the world, and toys from years ago — like Radio Flyer wagons, puddle jumpers, and mancala sets. The whole store was crammed with odd things that Mr. Magorium liked to call *whodathoughts*, *howsitgoes*, and *whatchamacallits*.

Winding stairs led up to a wide balcony at the back of the store. On the floor-to-ceiling shelves in the balcony was an awe-inspiring collection of children's books. Comfy couches and chairs welcomed readers who could sit for hours paging through the books. The tall, bald, Bellini, with his big handlebar mustache, kept it constantly stocked with all sorts of books. In fact, if a person asked for any book at all — Bellini would smile and somehow mysteriously produce it.

That morning, Eric was at the store before it was even open. He stood in front and waited for Molly Mahoney, the young woman who ran the store for Mr. Magorium, to arrive and unlock its tall, wide double doors.

He was so happy to be back, so filled with joy, he could hardly stand it. He did a little dance of delight and then tossed his hat into the air.

It was a good, high throw. The hat tumbled in mid-air . . . and then snagged on the corner of the sign above the door.

Oops!

One of his best hats! How would he ever get it down?

Eric stared up intently at the sign, wondering how to get his hat back. He didn't even notice that Molly Mahoney had walked up beside him. She took off her headphones as her face lit up with a smile. She was a pretty young woman in her twenties with short brown hair and large dark eyes. Eric liked her a lot because she always stopped to chat with him and gladly showed him anything in the store that he asked her about.

"Eric, you're back!" she cried, wrapping him in a warm, sisterly hug.

"Hi, Mahoney," he greeted her. Molly Mahoney liked to be called by her last name, Mahoney. Everyone called her that.

"I thought you were going away for four weeks," Mahoney recalled.

Eric looked away from her as he pulled out of the hug. Although he was glad to see her, he did not want to talk about camp. "No . . . it was just for two weeks," he lied.

"Did you make any friends?" she asked.

"Yeah . . . uh . . . one," he answered, still looking away. "Jeff."

Mahoney tilted her head. "Was he real?" she questioned.

"Yeah, sure," Eric replied.

"Was he an animal?" Mahoney asked with gentle suspicion.

Eric met her eyes at last and sighed. He couldn't fool her. "Jeff was a squirrel," he admitted. "How about you?" he asked, changing the subject. "Did you find a new job?"

Mahoney shrugged, and it was her turn to sigh. "I started looking," she replied.

Lately, Mahoney was beginning to wonder if working at Mr. Magorium's Wonder Emporium — as she had done ever since high school — was really a proper job for a grown-up. She had talked to Eric about this. Maybe it was time to look for something more . . . serious. However, she had no idea what that more serious, grown-up job should be.

"What were you staring at up there?" she asked, now also wanting to change the subject.

"My hat's stuck."

Looking up, Mahoney saw the cowboy hat with its

rattlesnake band sitting on top of the store's sign. It was about seven feet above the sidewalk. "You're going to need a ladder," she suggested.

"Naw," Eric disagreed as he began to back up. "I can jump up if I get a running start."

Mahoney smiled and shrugged in disbelief as she unlocked the store's front doors. Small bells jingled over the doorway.

Eric squared his shoulders and began to run. He knew that if he were anywhere else in the world, he could never jump high enough to reach his hat. No boy his size could have done it. But when he was at Mr. Magorium's place . . . anything was possible.

CHAPTER THREE

Mahoney left Eric outside and entered the store. She walked past a shelf of battery operated toys that magically sprang to life without even a touch. Mahoney put her key in the front register. As the cash drawer opened, the *ding!* sound it made alerted the rest of the toys that it was time to wake up. Music boxes began to play. The puppet theater pulled open its curtains. Windup toys sprang to life. Hovering kites ruffled their tails in an imaginary wind.

Mahoney looked at all this and smiled. "Good morning," she greeted the store brightly.

She then walked through the store to a massive oak

door toward the back. Beside the door was a dial. Around it were the words BALLS, TRUCKS, TRAINS, HOOPS, HOUSE. Carelessly she turned the dial without looking. She opened the oak door to a room filled with the world's most fantastic toy train set. Whistles blew and bells clanged as the electric trains passed above and below on tracks that intertwined one another. They passed through every possible climate from rain forest to arctic freeze.

With a quick glance, she saw that she had mistakenly turned the dial to TRAINS. It was not what she had meant to do. Shutting the door, Mahoney dialed again, this time carefully turning toward HOUSE. The door opened to reveal a set of wooden stairs leading upward. A large, old-fashioned lamp hung above her, lighting the way. At the top of the stairs was another landing and door. Mahoney banged the door's knocker.

An elderly man answered. Wild, white waves of hair framed his pleasant face. Bushy brows sat atop a pair of youthful dark eyes. He was wearing a yellow tuxedo shirt, tweed slacks, a blue blazer, and a pair of tennis shoes. "Mahoney!" he cried, greeting her with spirited cheer.

"Morning, Mr. Magorium," she said.

"Already?" he cried, surprised to learn the time of day. "Drat! Come in."

Mahoney stepped into Mr. Magorium's large and beautiful but very odd apartment. Around pieces of lovely old furniture sat unusual plastic modern sculptures. Masterpieces hung among framed fingerpaint paintings and colored pages from coloring books.

"How did you sleep?" Mahoney asked Mr. Magorium.

"Upside down," he replied, misunderstanding her question. "It made my feet tingly."

A zebra stood on one of the couches. He gazed dreamily out the window. "Mortimer! Get off the couch!" Mr. Magorium scolded mildly.

Mortimer simply turned toward Mr. Magorium, blinked at him, and then returned to his window watching.

"Or not," Mr. Magorium added with a shrug.

He suddenly turned to Mahoney. "Do you like turnips?"

"Nobody likes turnips," she replied, wrinkling her nose.

Mr. Magorium nodded thoughtfully. "So you probably wouldn't like turnip pudding," he concluded.

"Probably not," she agreed.

"Hmm . . . I wonder what I can do with all the turnip

pudding I made then," Mr. Magorium asked himself as he walked over to an end table and picked up a neatly folded stack of pajamas, a robe, and a pair of slippers.

Mahoney wasn't quite certain why he was talking about turnip pudding, but she had an important matter to discuss with him, so she got right to it. "Sir, I wanted to talk again about what we spoke about last week," she began.

"About how paper really shouldn't beat rock?" he asked.

"No, sir — about me possibly finding a new job," she reminded him.

"That's what I was saying," he agreed.

"What?" she asked.

"I spent all morning thinking — making turnip pudding and playing cat's cradle, which helps me think — and it occurred to me that I've owned the Emporium for over one hundred and thirteen years," he explained.

Mahoney nodded. It was no surprise to her that although Mr. Magorium did not look much older than 65, he was, in fact, 243 years old. He had often spoken to her of his travels and adventures. It seemed to Mahoney that he had seen and done practically everything that there was to see and do in the world.

"That's a very long time," he went on. "And, in all those years, I have never even looked at a sales receipt. So . . . I have absolutely no idea what the store is worth!"

"That's probably not very good," Mahoney said.

"Exactly!" he agreed, jabbing his index finger into the air. Mr. Magorium suddenly pulled a rubber ball from the pocket of his pants and pitched it across the room. "Mortimer! Fetch!" he shouted.

The zebra looked up lazily as the ball flew past him and then, once again, returned to looking out the window.

"Stupid zebra," Mr. Magorium grumbled to Mahoney. "Anyway," he said, getting back to his subject, "I'm hiring an accountant." As he said this, he slipped behind a beautiful Japanese screen where he began to change his clothes amidst a bevy of mirrors that swiveled and swung to show him his reflection.

"A . . . what?" Mahoney asked. She didn't know exactly what she'd been expecting him to say, but it certainly wasn't that.

"An accountant," Mr. Magorium repeated. "According to the name, I think it must be a cross between a counter and a mutant — and that may be exactly what we need. I've placed a call into some sort of agency and

they're sending one of their best mutants over some time today. You can consider the matter settled."

"How is the matter settled?" she asked.

"Quite perfectly, in my opinion," he replied as he stepped out from behind the screen, now wearing his pajamas, robe, and slippers. "Come with me," he said, and with an excited spring in his step, Mr. Magorium bounded into his kitchen. Mahoney hurried right behind him. The strange kitchen had rainbow walls and only one cupboard, which sat at an odd angle above the sink.

He pulled open the dishwasher. When the steam inside it cleared, it revealed a necktie, the game Risk, and a plain block of wood sitting in its racks. He pulled out the wooden block and handed it to Mahoney, presenting it with flair as though it were a great treasure. "This, my lovely . . . is for you."

Mahoney had no idea why he was giving her a block of wood! "Uh, thank you," she said. "What is it?"

Mr. Magorium beamed at her proudly. "It's the Congreve Cube!"

"It looks like a big block of wood," she pointed out.

"It is a big block of wood!" he agreed, nodding his head happily. "But now it's *your* big block of wood!"

Mahoney forced a thin smile to her lips. "Oh. Great.

I was just saying the other night: I don't have enough . . . blocks of wood." She really loved Mr. Magorium, even though he was the wackiest person she had ever known, and she didn't want to hurt his feelings.

Mr. Magorium's face grew serious. "Unlikely adventures require unlikely tools," he stated, looking with awed respect at the block of wood Mahoney held.

"Are we going on an adventure?" she asked hopefully.

"Oh, my dear, we're already on one," he replied. He cupped her face in his hands. "All I will say is that with faith, love, this block, and a counting mutant . . . you may find yourself somewhere you never imagined."

A crunching sound made him turn toward the refrigerator. Mortimer the Zebra had somehow opened the door and was browsing through, munching on whatever he liked. "Mortimer! Stay out of there!" Mr. Magorium shouted.

He smiled good-naturedly at Mahoney as he shooed the animal away. Mortimer could be a pest but she knew Mr. Magorium loved him dearly.

"And now, let's go the store," he said, heading for the door.

"Wait, sir," she stopped him, putting her hand on his shoulder. "You're wearing your pajamas."

Mr. Magorium looked down at himself quickly and saw she was right. "Oh, flapdoodle," he grumbled as he hurried off to his bedroom to get changed — again.

CHAPTER FOUR

Eric stood at the bottom of the stairs by the Door of Rooms as Mr. Magorium came down. He had on an orange striped tie over an orange shirt and orange pants. "Salutations, Eric!" Mr. Magorium greeted him. "Super hat."

"Thanks," Eric replied, proud that Mr. Magorium had noticed.

Mahoney came through the door right behind Mr. Magorium. She smiled at Eric. "Did you find a ladder?" she asked him.

"No, I just jumped up and got it," he said.

"That's got to be the highest a boy has ever jumped,"

Mahoney joked, not knowing that it was actually the truth.

"Ripping!" Mr. Magorium cheered.

That was what Eric loved about Mr. Magorium's Wonder Emporium — when he was there he felt like the most extraordinary kid on Earth. Everyone who came in felt that way. Even adults! Maybe it was because there was not an ordinary thing or person in the whole store.

It wasn't long before the Emporium was buzzing, bouncing, binging, whooping, and whirring with activity. Both children and adults filled the store, trying out all the fun and thrilling things there were to see. They never seemed to tire of the amazing toys, experiments, gizmos, inventions, and thingamabobs they discovered in Mr. Magorium's Wonder Emporium.

That day a customer asked for a hanging mobile, and Mr. Magorium showed her one made of real fish that magically floated in the air and blew bubbles as if they were actually underwater. When the woman complained that it cost too much, he showed her a cheaper mobile made of frozen fish sticks.

Mahoney sat at the front counter coloring with Eric. She admired the orange trees and purple sky that he colored.

A kindly-looking grandmother came by to ask

Mahoney about a gift for her grandson's birthday. "All he wants is a shiny red fire engine with the ladder that goes up and the hose that squirts water," she explained, "but I can't find one."

"Sounds like a job for *The Big Book*," Mahoney told the grandmother. Eric smiled excitedly. He loved when Mahoney used *The Big Book*.

She pulled a large book from the shelf behind her. It had a worn leather cover and appeared to be as old as Mr. Magorium himself. "This contains all the toys we have in stock," she said. "Let's try F."

The fat, old book had lettered tabs that marked each section alphabetically. Mahoney grasped the F tab and pulled the book open. Inside, in an open, cutaway space, sat the exact fire engine the grandmother had described! "How did you do that?" the elderly woman gasped.

"It's the book," Mahoney explained with a smile. "It's magic."

Eric went back to his coloring while Mahoney wrapped the fire engine for the grandmother. She stopped working for a moment to watch a boy dance along the store wearing a Chinese New Year's dragon on his head, but then was startled by the man who came up quietly behind her.

"Uh, hello, miss," the man said.

Eric looked up from his coloring to see the man. He was very average-looking, neatly dressed in a gray suit with a light gray shirt and a gray striped tie. His short hair was neatly combed. In his hand he clutched a briefcase. "I'm Henry Weston. I'm an accountant and I'm here for an interview."

"Hi," she greeted him. "I'm Mahoney, the store manager. I'll go get Mr. Magorium for you."

Eric trailed behind her as they went to the back of the store. They found Mr. Magorium juggling three brightly colored balls in the air. A crowd of children and their parents surrounded him. They were amazed at his talent.

"Sir? The mutant is here," Mahoney told him.

Mr. Magorium smiled. His three juggling balls flew into the air and magically disappeared.

Mr. Magorium hopped around excitedly. Then he settled down and straightened his tie. "Do I look like I own this store?" he asked Mahoney, "or do I look like me?"

"Sir, you're fine," Mahoney told him. "Calm down."

"I've never met an accountant before," he said, explaining his case of jittery nerves.

"Sir, they're just like us," Mahoney told him.

Mahoney, Eric, and Mr. Magorium hurried through the store to the front counter where Henry Weston, the

accountant, stood waiting. Mr. Magorium extended his hand to the accountant. "Greetings!" he said. "Edward Magorium: toy impresario, wonder aficionado, avid shoe wearer. You're here for the accounting position?"

"Yes, yes," Henry Weston replied. He introduced himself and shook Mr. Magorium's hand.

"Since you are good at counting things, I have a question for you," Mr. Magorium said to Henry. "Why, for the love of mustard, are there never enough hotdog buns in a package?"

Eric scratched his head thoughtfully. That did seem to be true. There were always fewer buns in the bun package than hotdogs in the hotdog package. He decided this might be an interesting discussion and settled down beside a cabinet a little way away to listen.

"Maybe there are extra hotdogs," Henry suggested.

"But why?" Mr. Magorium pressed him to explain.

Henry thought about this before he answered. "I think . . . maybe . . . if you drop two hotdogs . . ."

"What kind of insufferable fool drops a hotdog?" Mr. Magorium asked, unable to imagine anyone being that careless with something as wonderful as a hotdog.

Henry looked confused. "I don't know. I mean, anything can happen."

Mr. Magorium's face lit up with delight as he repeated

Henry's words. "Anything can happen! How absolutely true!" He looked Henry up and down approvingly. "You're exactly the mutant I'm looking for. You're hired!"

Mr. Magorium beckoned for Henry to follow him. "Come with me. I've heard wonderful things about you."

"Really?" Henry questioned, finding this hard to believe. After all, he didn't know anyone Mr. Magorium knew.

"No. Not yet," Mr. Magorium admitted. "But I'm sure I will." He noticed the briefcase Henry held. "Oh, good, you brought your own abacus! Top notch! I'll show you the office."

On their way to the office, Mr. Magorium proudly showed Henry around the store, gesturing at its stunning variety of toys. He explained to the accountant, "We sell almost every kind of whatnot imaginable, Mutant, from ant farms to zeppelins."

Incredible things were happening all around them as they weaved their way through the store. A game of duck duck goose was being played with an actual goose. Eric was balancing an impossibly tall stack of oddly-shaped boxes in one hand. And from a wall chock full of stuffed animals, a single sock monkey puppet reached out longingly to Henry with its arms outstretched.

Henry, however, was completely unaware of the magic surrounding him and noticed none of it.

Mr. Magorium explained a bit of the history of the store to Henry as they walked, "I've owned this store for one hundred and thirteen years, since I came to this country," he started. "Although I've been inventing toys since the mid-1770s."

"Excuse me?" Henry sputtered in disbelief. "Did you say 1770s? That would mean you're at least *two hundred and thirty seven years old*!"

At this Mr. Magorium stopped abruptly and scolded Henry, "You're already hired, mutant. There's no need to show off."

Henry looked at Mr. Magorium and the store suspiciously with squinted eyes. *What was going on here?* he wondered.

CHAPTER FIVE

Mahoney was at the front counter ringing up an order for a customer. The customer was a young man about her own age. As she waited for him to get out his payment, her fingers danced along the counter as though she were playing her piano. It was a habit she'd had ever since she was a child and had first started playing. The customer looked at her as if seeing her for the first time. "Molly? Molly Mahoney?" he asked.

"Yeah . . ." she replied, a bit confused. How did he know her name?

He beamed a smile. "I'm Dave Wolf. I was in your physics class in college."

"Oh, hey," she greeted him politely, remembering him only slightly.

"Hey . . . holy cow! You worked here during college. You still work here!"

Mahoney blushed, feeling funny about not having gone on to a more grown-up-seeming job. "Yeah . . . I mean . . . well, yeah. Actually, I've worked here since high school."

"When did you finish college?" Dave Wolf asked.

"I didn't, actually," she admitted. It made her think of all the other things she hadn't finished. Finishing things was something she had never had much success with. But she pushed the thought away and tried to change the topic. "How about you? What are you up to?"

"I'm an engineer," he replied.

"Cool!" Mahoney said. "How big is your train?" she joked.

Dave Wolf looked puzzled at first, but then he laughed. "I get it! Funny!"

"So . . . an engineer," she said, trying to make small talk.

"Yeah," he agreed, nodding. "Married. Baby on the way."

"Wow," she said.

"Yeah . . . all grown-up," he added. "I never would have recognized you except for that thing you do with your fingers. Do you still play the piano?"

"I do," she said. "Every day."

"Where are you playing?" he asked.

At first she didn't understand what he meant. Then it hit her. He thought she played at a club or concert hall, or even a restaurant — somewhere that he could go to hear her perform.

She was too honest to lie about it. "My apartment," she mumbled.

There was a moment where neither of them knew what to say next. At last, Dave Wolf took his package from the counter and began to back away. "It was nice to see you again," he said. "I always wondered what happened to you."

Mahoney laughed uncomfortably. "Well . . . not much," she said.

He was about to go when Mahoney noticed something moving around in his bag — something that did not belong there. "I'm sorry, Dave," Mahoney said, coming out from behind the counter. "Hold on a second." She looked into his bag and saw just what she had suspected. "Come on," she commanded, speaking sternly into the bag. "Get out of there."

Suddenly a Super Ball shot up out of the bag and bounced right into Mahoney's hand. "You, too," she demanded, still talking to something inside the bag. A second Super Ball sprang out of the bag. Mahoney caught it as well.

"Super Balls," she apologized to her old classmate. "They're always trying to escape."

Looking frightened, he quickly left the store. Mahoney sighed. As she turned back to the counter, she noticed two young boys staring at her. "You're amazing!" one of them said to her.

She wished she could say she'd done something magical and clever. But it was the Super Balls that had flown through the air on their own. She had nothing to do with it.

"No," she said to the boy. "It's not me."

CHAPTER SIX

Here we are," Mr. Magorium said to Henry. He flipped on a light in an office at the back of the store. "I haven't thrown anything away!" he added proudly.

"Yes. Yes. I can see that," Henry said. It was by far the messiest room Henry had ever seen. Pages of different sizes and shapes were everywhere, sitting high in stacks that looked like they might topple over at any moment. "Are these all receipts?" he asked.

"Mostly," Mr. Magorium said. "I believe some are IOUs and invoices and such. Some might be doodles that I never framed. I can't tell."

Henry saw that he would have a lot of work to do.

From the look of things he doubted that Mr. Magorium had ever kept an account of his income. He had probably never even filed a tax return or applied for a city business license.

"Mr. Magorium," he began, "you realize that sorting through this . . ." — he spread his arms wide, trying to come up with a word to describe the incredible mess laid out before him — ". . . this fire hazard will be a giant task. Since so far you've managed to keep from going bankrupt, being thrown out for not having a license, or sent to jail for not paying your taxes — why do you want to do this now?"

"Can you keep a secret?" Mr. Magorium asked.

"Yes," Henry replied.

"I'm leaving."

"You're leaving the store?" Henry questioned.

"The world." Mr. Magorium looked at Henry to see if he understood his meaning and wasn't sure that the young mutant did. So he explained: "You see these shoes?" he said, lifting his right foot to show Henry a pair of brown leather shoes. "I found these in a tiny shop in Italy and fell in love with them so entirely that I bought enough pairs to last my whole life." He gazed meaningfully into Henry's eyes. "These are my last pair."

Mr. Magorium could tell from Henry's serious

expression that he now understood what Mr. Magorium was saying. They shared a silent moment. "Now, if you'll excuse me," Mr. Magorium said, breaking the silence. "I have a pressing marbles match at noon and must warm my thumbs."

Eric could hardly wait for Mr. Magorium to come out of his office. There was something odd in the store that Mr. Magorium needed to see — and right away.

At last, Mr. Magorium came through the door, flexing his thumbs, preparing for his marbles match. Eric stepped in front of him. "Mr. Magorium," he said. "There's something I have to show you."

Mr. Magorium's bushy brows furrowed in concern and he followed Eric to a corner of the Air & Space section. Eric had noticed the problem just a little while ago while he was checking out the new windup UFOs with flashing rainbow lights.

"Does this seem right to you?" Eric asked. A small corner of the brightly colored Air & Space section was now an ashy, dull shade. Every color in that particular corner had faded to gray!

"No. It doesn't seem right at all," Mr. Magorium agreed seriously.

Eric turned toward the window in the door to the office. Inside the office, Henry stood scratching his head as though he were puzzled about something. Right away, Eric noticed that Henry's gray suit matched the gray patch in the corner of the store perfectly! It was the exact same shade of gray!

Both Eric and Mr. Magorium looked at Henry, back at the gray corner, and then again at Henry in his gray suit. "We must keep a watchful eye on this, Eric," Mr. Magorium said.

That evening, Eric arrived home before his mother returned from work. He decided to complete a project he'd been working on before he left for camp, a clock made from a lemon. Outside his window, he heard the sound of children playing. Walking to the window, he watched them. His mother told him to make friends. He'd said he would. But he'd been so concerned today about the gray spot in the store that he'd forgotten all about trying to befriend any of the children who came in. The only people he'd spoken to were Mahoney and Mr. Magorium. They were his friends. But they weren't the kind of friends his mother had in mind.

His mother had meant friends his own age — kids like the ones outside. Why didn't he go out and play with those kids? He didn't know why. Was he scared that they wouldn't like him? He wasn't sure. But something always seemed to hold him back.

There were lots of kids at Mr. Magorium's place. Tomorrow he would make a real effort to play with them.

He headed for his room to select a new hat to wear. It had to be one that not only Mr. Magorium would like but also one that his new friends wouldn't think was too strange.

CHAPTER SEVEN

The next morning, Eric entered the Lincoln Log area of the store wearing his best Mexican sombrero. Its large brim drooped over his face but he didn't mind. The brim would help cover the shyness he felt. And maybe some kid would come along to ask him where he'd gotten it. Eric could tell all about the trip he'd taken to Mexico with his mother last winter. They'd talk and become friends. It might happen.

A group of children were already there building small houses with the Lincoln Logs. Eric stood by watching, waiting for someone to invite him to play or at least ask about his hat.

Some of the kids stared at him curiously but none of them invited him to join them. Not sure what else to do, Eric went to the barrel of wooden logs and scooped out a large handful for himself in another corner of the play area.

He noticed Henry looking in at him. He was red-faced and seemed upset. Today he had on another gray suit, different but just as gray as the suit he'd worn yesterday. He stopped for a moment to look at Eric and the other children before moving on.

While Eric built with Lincoln Logs, Mr. Magorium was still thinking about the unhealthy-looking gray spot in his store. What could be causing it?

Hoping to find an answer, he climbed to the store's book balcony. He took out a tiny book he thought might give him some information but as soon as he opened it, Henry climbed into the balcony. He looked very upset. "Mr. Magorium, we have a few serious problems," Henry said. "According to your employment records, you've had several make-believe, fictional characters working for you!"

"Like whom?" Mr. Magorium asked, closing his tiny book.

"A king of some alien planet," Henry reported.

"He's not fictional," Mr. Magorium pointed out. "He's not actually the king, but he's not fictional."

"What about Bellini?" Henry asked, trying not to sound as frustrated with Mr. Magorium as he was feeling. "Who is he?"

"Bellini is the book builder who lives in the basement." Mr. Magorium nodded at his vast collection of children's books. "Just ask him for any book and Bellini will produce it. Doesn't he do a wonderful job?"

"You have someone living in your basement?!" Henry cried. He'd had no idea!

"He was born there. I certainly can't ask him to leave," Mr. Magorium insisted. At that moment a very tall, bald-headed man in a heavy apron walked by carrying a stack of books. It was Bellini, the man in charge of the books at the store. Mr. Magorium nodded at him as if to say: *See, he's real enough.*

"What about this invoice sent from a company in Brazil that says you owe three hundred thousand *real* for a magic doorknob?" Henry asked.

Mr. Magorium waved his hand. "That's ridiculous."

"Thank you," Henry said, relieved.

"Who charges that much for a magic doorknob?" Mr. Magorium added. "I can get a magic doorknob for half that price."

Henry's shoulders slumped. Sorting out Mr. Magorium's Magic Emporium seemed like it was going to be impossible! He was beginning to wish he'd never agreed to take the job in the first place.

Eric kept building with his Lincoln Logs. Even as he worked, he could not get his mind off the problem of making friends. It seemed to come so naturally to other kids. They just went ahead and played together. Why wasn't it easy for him? He knew why, really. He thought about it too much. Would they like him? Would he like them?

He didn't always want to do what the other kids were doing, either. The Lincoln Logs were a good example of this. If he had wanted to make dinky little Lincoln Log houses, he could have joined the other kids. But Lincoln Logs were too cool for building simple stuff. Why not build something more interesting? Would Lincoln, the great man himself, have thought making little cabins from the blocks named after him was interesting?

Thinking of Abraham Lincoln gave Eric a great idea. Why not build a statue of Lincoln? Now that was interesting!

This project made Eric excited. He forgot about

everything else — the gray spot in the store, the problem of making friends — and threw all his energy into it. After a while, he had the sense that people were watching him. His Lincoln Log Lincoln was attracting an audience!

When he had put on the last log, completing Lincoln's tall stovepipe hat, he turned around. Adults and children all stood in a circle watching. But instead of feeling proud, Eric was overcome with the awkward feeling that they all thought he was weird. "Oh, sorry," he murmured to the crowd. "I sort of took over. Sorry. Sorry." He backed away, embarrassed.

Stuffing a wad of receipts into his briefcase, Henry prepared to leave the store and work more at home. Walking through the store, he passed a Lincoln Log building station. It was crowded with adults and children marveling at a life-sized figure of Abraham Lincoln!

Henry stopped to stare it. He stood next to Eric, in his very large sombrero. "Who did that?" Henry asked Eric.

"I did," Eric told him.

It was impossible! How could such a young boy build something so difficult out of simple Lincoln Logs? "No! Seriously, who helped?" Henry asked.

Eric shook his head. "Nobody."

Henry stared down at Eric. Could it be true? What an odd but talented kid, he thought.

He suddenly noticed Mahoney leaving the store through the front door. She seemed like a sensible girl — sort of. He had questions he needed to ask her. "Wait!" he called, hurrying toward her.

He caught up with her out on the street. "I need your help," he said frantically. "I need you to explain to me about this . . . history . . . he's made up out of these receipts."

"What history?" Mahoney asked.

Henry opened his briefcase and took out some of the receipts. He showed her the first one he picked out of the batch. "Look at this! It's a signed IOU from Thomas Edison! Does that seem like something that would exist in the real world?"

Mahoney was interested. She didn't know Mr. Magorium had an IOU from the man who invented the lightbulb!

"'P.S. Thanks for the idea!'" Henry read. "It has a picture of a lightbulb next to it!"

"Is that for real?" Mahoney asked, laughing lightly. It was so cool!

"No!" Henry shouted. "How could that be real?"

"Well," Mahoney considered, studying the paper. "It does have his signature on it."

Henry slumped onto a nearby bench. "Please, I need a simple explanation."

"Sure. It's a magical toy store," Mahoney explained.

"There's no such thing as a magical toy store!" Henry argued.

"Of course there is. This *is* one," Mahoney insisted.

"Do you expect me to believe that this store sitting right behind me is magical?" he demanded.

Mahoney put her hands on her hips in annoyance. He was the most unimaginative person she had ever met! "Well, it's magical whether you believe it or not!"

"Okay, when you say magical, do you mean special?" he asked.

"I mean magical," she said firmly.

"Unique?" he suggested.

"Magical," she repeated.

"Really, really cool?" he tried.

"No! Magical!"

Henry sighed deeply. "Magical. Right. Listen, I'm sorry but to me, it's just a toy store."

"I knew it as soon as I saw the suit," she said.

"Knew what?" Henry asked.

"You're a 'just' guy. Everything to you is 'just' this or

'just' that," she explained angrily. "This is 'just' a drawing. This is 'just' some food. This is 'just' what it is, nothing more."

Henry's arm waved toward Mr. Magorium's Wonder Emporium. "But this is *just* a store!"

"I'm sure to you it is!" Mahoney shouted at him. She couldn't recall ever being angrier with anyone! "That's why you are what you are!"

Henry stood up and faced her. "What I am, Ms. Mahoney, is a grown-up. As much as I appreciate your childlike outlook and pixieish charm, the truth is, I grew out of that a long time ago! Honestly, I'm a little surprised that you haven't! But you get to spend your time here, and I get to spend my time in reality. A reality I'm looking forward to returning to." He strode purposefully past her. "Excuse me," he huffed as he walked toward his bus stop. "I have work to do."

CHAPTER EIGHT

Mahoney came into her half-painted front hall and dropped her bag onto the floor. Trudging over to her couch, she threw herself onto it. She'd had a bad day — one of the worst she could remember in recent times. Meeting her former classmate had made her feel like a child, as though she'd somehow forgotten to grow up. But her fight with Henry had made her feel even worse!

Was what he said true?

Was she living in a make-believe dream world?

Getting off the couch, she went to the piano and began to play. She threw all her energy into the piece of music. Maybe this time she'd get past the part of the music where she always stopped and didn't know what to play next. Perhaps this was the moment when she would finally finish the song she'd been trying to play since she was a girl . . . .

She played with gusto, the notes growing louder and louder . . . until suddenly — she stopped. At the same spot she always did. Mahoney simply could not play what came next.

The block of wood Mr. Magorium had given to her sat on her table. She stopped to look at it. What had Mr. Magorium called it — the Congreve Cube? It was probably just a plain block of wood. And Mr. Magorium was probably just a lovable but loony old guy.

That same evening, Eric was at home eating dinner with his mother. It was a quiet dinner. The only sound was their chewing and the sound of pages turning. His mother, still in her suit from work, was going over her business papers. Eric was involved in his book, *Robinson Crusoe*, about a man who had washed ashore on a desert island.

His mother looked up from her papers. "Sweetheart, did you spend the whole day at the store?" she asked.

He looked up and swallowed with a gulp. How did she know that? She had probably guessed, but she'd guessed right.

Eric knew how she felt, so he tried to present his day in a positive way. "I built a sculpture, and got twenty thousand paddles in paddle ball, and I figured out how to win at solitaire without cheating."

His mother looked at him, her eyes filled with concern. "Eric, those are all things you do by yourself," she remarked.

"No . . . there were people around," he said.

"Sweetheart, we agreed that you could come back from camp early if you made an effort to make some friends."

"It's not my fault," Eric argued. "People don't like me."

His mother shook her head. "People *love* you once they get a chance to know you."

"No, they don't," Eric insisted. "They think I'm weird."

"Just because you build sculptures by yourself?" she asked.

"Because nobody wants to play with me!" he shouted.

His mother didn't exactly shout back, but she raised

her voice slightly. "Have you asked anyone to play with you?"

Eric hung his head. "Not really."

"Well, Eric, you have to give people a chance," his mother advised. "Just pick someone, anyone. Pick someone you don't know and try to make friends. See what happens. Start by saying hi."

Mr. Magorium walked around his store. He picked up a paper airplane and admired it. He loved his store, but he was also worried about it. The Emporium was not acting as he expected. "I must say," he spoke to the store, "I am very disappointed in you."

With a flick of his wrist, he sent the paper plane soaring around the store. "I understand feeling sad," he went on, "or scared or even doubtful, but there is no reason to turn gray and start pouting." After a day of thinking hard about the problem, that was what Mr. Magorium had decided. The gray spot in the store had shown up because the store was unhappy. It knew that he was planning to leave.

He sat on a piano bench and spoke seriously to the store. "The truth is that I am leaving tomorrow and Mahoney, bless her timid heart, will be given care of you.

I'm sorry my sweet, but it is a perfect fact and no amount of misbehavior will change it."

He knew the store was already sad so he made his tone gentler. "Mahoney loves you," he told the store. "As do I and we must face tomorrow with determination, joy, and bravery."

The paper airplane came to rest right at Mr. Magorium's feet. He picked it up lovingly. He would miss the store and all the toys who were friends to him. But the time had come for him to leave the world; after all, two-hundred-and-forty-three years were more than most people were given. "I expect you to pull yourself together and put your best face on by the time of my departure," he finished, with a small sniff.

Mr. Magorium knew he was leaving, no matter how anyone felt about it. If he could leave everything as he hoped it would be — then he wouldn't mind leaving at all.

CHAPTER NINE

In the morning, Eric selected his red fez hat to wear to the store. It was simple, round with no brim. He liked the way its black tassel bounced around when he walked.

Although Mahoney had greeted him with a smile, she was busy setting up and could not play with him. There were no other children there.

He strolled toward the back of the store. Through the window in the office door, Eric noticed someone inside. Peering in, he saw Henry sitting at his desk in the messy office full of papers.

Eric remembered the advice his mother had given

him. Start by saying hi. He ran to the art section and got a large pad and crayons. He scrawled the word HI on the paper. Running back to the office, he held the paper up to the window.

Henry read the note and waved.

Taking the wave as a good sign, Eric wrote on another sheet: I'M ERIC. DO YOU LIKE CHECKERS?

Henry scribbled on one of the scrap sheets on his desk and held his reply up for Eric to see: I DID WHEN I WAS A KID.

Eric turned his paper over and wrote quickly. He held it to the window. DO YOU WANT TO PLAY?

I HAVE TO WORK, Henry's sign replied.

AFTER WORK? Eric wrote.

I NEVER STOP WORKING, Henry told him in a sign.

THAT'S SAD. It was Eric's last sign before he walked away. His first try at making a friend had failed. Disappointed, he scooped up a ball from a bin and bounced it.

Mr. Magorium bounded out from the Door of Rooms stairway. "Eric!" he greeted him brightly.

"Morning, sir."

Eric trailed Mr. Magorium as he joined Mahoney in the Air & Space section. The gray corner was still gray and the gray spot was larger than it had been the day before. “Sir, what’s wrong with this corner?” Mahoney asked Mr. Magorium.

“Sadness. Confusion,” he replied. “Apparently the store is not taking my departure well.”

Mahoney also looked confused. So did Eric. “What departure?” she asked.

“It was meant to be a stunning surprise,” Mr. Magorium explained. “But the store has other ideas so I must tell you now. I’m giving you the store!”

Mahoney’s eyes widened in shock. “You’re giving me the store?” she gasped.

“Surprise!” Mr. Magorium sang out.

“Sir, I can’t take the Emporium,” Mahoney objected.

“But you need it!” Mr. Magorium insisted. “You told me you needed a new job, a different occupation.”

“I meant teaching music, not owning the Emporium,” she replied. “You have to run the store. It’s Mr. Magorium’s Wonder Emporium. It rhymes! Besides, you’re magic —and I’m not.”

Before Mahoney could say anything more, a small boy came up alongside her and tugged on her shirt. He was looking for a book, a copy of *Curious George Goes to the Hospital.*

"An excellent piece of literature!" Mr. Magorium commented.

"Have you read it?" the boy asked.

"Read it?" Mr. Magorium cried. "I've even had brunch with The Man in the Yellow Hat!"

Mahoney went to the store's intercom — a brass cup on the end of a metal tube mounted on the wall — and spoke to Bellini. "Bellini, *Curious George Goes to the Hospital* please," she requested. "Thank you."

In minutes a door slid open and Bellini emerged holding the Curious George book and several others. Mahoney pointed out the boy who had requested it and Bellini handed the book to him.

The boy wandered away to look at the book and Eric walked off to think about what Mr. Magorium had said. Was he really giving the store to Mahoney?

He watched them stand by the front counter and continued to argue. As he watched, he noticed something interesting — and disturbing. Every time Mahoney protested that she did not want the store, the gray spot in the Air & Space corner grew larger . . . and larger . . . and larger still.

As Eric roamed through the store he saw more disturbing things. Some children had done colorful finger

paintings that were hanging on a clothes line to dry. As they dried they faded and grew gray.

The gray kept expanding, creeping along the walls and shelves. One shelf collapsed with a *CRASH* under the weight of so much gray gloom.

Mr. Magorium and Mahoney stopped their argument when they heard the sound of the crashing shelf.

The little boy who had asked for the Curious George book approached Mahoney and Mr. Magorium. "Excuse me," he began, holding the book up for them. "There's something wrong with the book you gave me."

Mr. Magorium opened the book. All the letters were jumbled. The pictures were only half finished. "I see. I'll notify Bellini right away," he told the boy.

Mr. Magorium and Mahoney ran to the dial that opened the Door of Rooms. Mr. Magorium turned it to TRAINS. When he opened the door, only the stairs were on the other side. "Confound it!" Mr. Magorium cried, looking worried. "Mahoney, check *The Big Book*."

They ran back to the front counter where *The Big Book* was shelved. "I would like a lollipop," Mahoney told the book. She grabbed the L tab and pulled the book open.

A lemur jumped out!

The furry creature leaped off the counter and began

to race around the store. Mr. Magorium went to the paper airplane display. He tossed a plane. It instantly fell to his feet. He threw a second plane. It dropped as well. "Mahoney!" he cried anxiously. "The laws of gravity have begun to apply!"

"I asked *The Big Book* for a lollipop and I got a lemur!" she told him.

"A lemur?! We don't even carry lemurs!" Mr. Magorium was very distressed. "I'm not even sure if I know what a lemur is! Wait! Is it the little primate thing? Kind of looks like a raccoon, kind of like a —"

"Sir," Mahoney interrupted him. "We don't have time to —"

"We don't have time to discuss lemurs!" Mr. Magorium finished for her. "You're right! Where's Eric?"

Eric had gone off to test the Super Balls. Every one he tried to bounce simply lay on the floor, refusing to move.

Eric heard Mr. Magorium call for him. Leaving the super balls, he ran through the store toward him. Everywhere he looked, things where in chaos. The model airplanes were dive-bombing customers, sending them screaming in all directions. A plume of smoke was rising from the Air & Space section. The lemur had jumped onto a boy's back, and the boy was crying out in terror. A stuffed dragon had begun breathing real fire!

He had to do something!

He climbed up on the front counter and announced in his most official sounding voice: "The store is undergoing a little difficulty right now," he said loudly. "Please leave through the front door calmly and in an orderly fashion. . . . And maybe try to avoid the slimy guy," he added as a person dripping in green goo ran by.

He was interrupted by a kite flying around his head. It buzzed the top of his hair, and he batted it out of his way.

A woman approached. She was soaking wet and had seaweed hanging from her clothing and a squid sitting atop her head. She held a book up to Eric. "I am very disappointed with this copy of *Explore the Sea,*" she complained.

Things were totally out of control! What could ever fix such a mess? He looked for Mr. Magorium and found him by the Door of Rooms waving his arms. He wanted them all to follow him up the stairs. Eric sure hoped he had some kind of plan.

CHAPTER TEN

As soon as Eric and Mahoney got everyone out of the store, Mr. Magorium called an emergency meeting in his apartment. Henry was there and so were assorted dolls and toys, all sitting around a long table. Mortimer the zebra watched it from his spot on the couch.

Mr. Magorium pounded the table with a judge's gavel that squeaked each time it hit. "Order, order!" he proclaimed. "Now, the first order of business, Eric . . ."

Eric sat at attention, waiting.

"Ingenious hat," Mr. Magorium complimented him.

Eric lightly touched the round fez hat he still wore on his head. "Thank you, sir."

"Second order of business," Mr. Magorium continued. "The store is stunningly upset as indicated by its temper tantrum."

"What temper tantrum?" Henry asked.

"You didn't see it? How could you not have seen it?" Mr. Magorium asked in disbelief.

"He was in his office," Eric explained.

"Ah. I see," Mr. Magorium said, nodding at Eric and Henry. "Well, the store went a bit . . . awry, a little crazy." He folded his arms and then unfolded them. "You see, it is my belief that the store has been growing increasingly sad and today threw a fit."

"Like a temper tantrum?" Mahoney asked him.

"Precisely," he agreed. "I have given the store the same attitude, imagination, and emotion as the children who come to play in it. And, as such, it is prone to the same outbursts as its clients."

"Maybe it needs a timeout," Eric suggested.

"Wait," Henry spoke up, clearly bewildered by what he was hearing. "I'm sorry but . . . how could a store throw a temper tantrum?"

It was Mr. Magorium's turn to look astonished. He looked to Mahoney and Eric, even to the dolls and toys. "Did no one explain to the mutant that it's a magical toy store?" he asked.

"I tried," Mahoney said.

Mr. Magorium leaned toward Henry. "It's a magical toy store, Mutant. It can do all sorts of things."

"But it didn't start turning gray until Henry showed up," Eric pointed out.

"Me?" Henry gasped.

"I realize that, Eric," Mr. Magorium replied.

"Listen," Henry spoke angrily. "If I'm making your toy store go on the fritz, I can submit a form to request another accounting agent."

"Does your whole job consist of submitting forms?" Mahoney snapped at him irritably.

"No," he snapped back. "Sometimes I *receive* forms."

"Order! Order!" Mr. Magorium banged the table with his squeaking gavel.

Henry continued to argue with Mahoney. "I am not responsible for whatever happened in the Emporium today," he insisted angrily. "I was just in the office working."

"There's that 'just' word again," Mahoney pointed out.

Henry leaned in toward her, red-faced with anger. "Will you give it up for just —"

Mahoney laughed disdainfully when he said the word *just* yet again.

Mr. Magorium's gavel squeaked even louder. "Enough!" he shouted. "Although Henry's presence has coincided with the store's dismay, it is not the cause," he declared. "He is only here to determine my legacy to Mahoney."

"What do you mean by your *legacy*?" Mahoney asked.

"The Emporium is my legacy to you," Mr. Magorium explained to her.

"You mean Mahoney gets to run the store?" Eric shouted excitedly. "How cool!"

"And now the store is worried that she may not want it," Mr. Magorium went on.

Eric found this unbelievable. "Mahoney, why wouldn't you want the store?"

"But why are you giving me the store?" Mahoney asked Mr. Magorium.

Mr. Magorium smiled sweetly. "I told you, my dear, I am leaving."

"I thought you meant a trip or a vacation!" Mahoney said, rising from her seat, alarmed. "What kind of leaving are you talking about?"

Mr. Magorium didn't reply, but Eric somehow knew what he meant. He could tell by the serious expression in Mr. Magorium's eyes. "Mahoney," Eric spoke gently,

"Mr. Magorium is going to heaven." He looked to Mr. Magorium to confirm this. "Right?"

"Heaven. Elysium. Shangri-La. Perhaps I may return as a bumblebee," Mr. Magorium mused.

Mahoney's eyes filled with tears. "Are you dying?" she asked.

"Lightbulbs die, my sweet. I will depart," he replied.

"Are you sick?" she asked him.

"Not necessarily," he said.

"Not necessarily!" she repeated, now very upset. "When exactly were you planning to depart?"

"Around four-thirty tomorrow," Mr. Magorium answered, checking his watch.

CHAPTER ELEVEN

Mahoney ran from the table and called for an ambulance. When the emergency medical technicians came, she made up a story. She told them Mr. Magorium was breathing heavily, that he was out of his mind — delusional.

They rushed him to hospital and Mahoney went along. She told the doctors that Mr. Magorium had lost his mind. "He claims he owns a magical toy store," she said to them.

"I do," Mr. Magorium insisted as they strapped him into a hospital gurney.

"He thinks he's a two-hundred-and-forty-two-year-old man," she continued.

"I am not two-hundred-and-forty-two!" Mr. Magorium objected. "I am two-hundred-and-forty-three! You were at my party, Mahoney! You brought balloons."

The doctors did not have to hear any more to be convinced that Mr. Magorium was not in his right mind. With his hospital bed still out in the hall, they stood around him, observing Mr. Magorium carefully.

"He may have had a stroke," one of them suggested. Mr. Magorium was outraged by the idea. "The only stroke I have ever had is a stroke of genius!" he said.

"Nurse, get him some medicine to calm him down," one of the doctors said to a passing nurse. The nurse went for the medicine and the doctors walked off into a corner to discuss Mr. Magorium's case.

Mr. Magorium turned toward Mahoney. "Why are you lying like this?" he asked.

"I have to," she replied.

"But your pants will catch fire," he reminded her.

"I don't care, sir. I'm not letting you go. You have to live!" she told him.

Mr. Magorium patted her hand soothingly. "Darling, I have lived."

The nurse returned with a large needle in her hand and gave it to one of the doctors who had returned to Mr. Magorium's bedside. The doctor gave Mr. Magorium a shot. "You're going to get a little sleepy," the doctor warned.

"My dear man," said Mr. Magorium, "if you think a complex and amazing machine such as my arterial system is going to give in to your . . ." Mr. Magorium never finished his sentence because in the next half second he was sleeping soundly.

Hospital attendants arrived and rolled him through double doors to a patients-only room where Mahoney was forbidden to follow. As she stood there, not knowing what to do next, Henry came alongside her. "Sorry," he said to her kindly. "I know this is hard."

"Thanks," she said.

"I was searching for his medical insurance and I haven't been able to find anything," he told her. "Hospital bills are very expensive these days so I'm a little worried."

Mahoney's eyes flashed with fury. Mr. Magorium was *dying* — and all he could think about were *medical bills*! "Maybe you should just go home!" she snarled at him.

"What? I'm trying to be helpful," he defended himself.

"Well, you're being positively dreadful," she scolded.

"I'm sorry," he apologized.

"I know," she said, softening because he looked so defeated. "It's okay. Go home."

He nodded helplessly. "I'll see you back at the store," he said.

"Okay," she agreed.

He patted her on the shoulder before walking off down the hallway. On the way out, he nodded to Eric, who was coming toward Mahoney holding a paper bag.

Eric sized up the situation quickly. He could tell from their unhappy faces that Mahoney and the mutant had been fighting again. "You know, you shouldn't be so hard on the mutant," he said when he reached her.

"He wants to talk about insurance!" she exploded. "Now!"

"I know, but it's the only thing he knows how to talk about," Eric explained.

Mahoney wrapped her arm around Eric and sighed deeply. "What are we going to do?"

"I don't know," Eric replied. "But right now Mr. Magorium has another problem." He opened the bag to show her the things he'd packed. "He doesn't have any pajamas."

In about two hours, a doctor came back through the double doors and found Mahoney sitting with Eric in

the hallway. He told them that they could go in to see Mr. Magorium.

As they walked down the hall, the doctor told them that they had run tests but couldn't find anything wrong with Mr. Magorium.

When they went in to see Mr. Magorium, he was awake. He was not at all surprised to hear that he was in perfect health. "If you're so healthy, why are you leaving?" Mahoney asked him.

"It's my time to go," he answered patiently.

"But what are we going to do without you?" she asked.

"Run the store," he replied.

Mahoney threw her arms out at her side. Why couldn't she get through to him? "Sir, I don't know how!"

"That's why I gave you the Congreve Cube," he explained.

"The block of wood?" Mahoney questioned.

"Yes."

"But it just sits there," she said.

"What have you done with it?" he asked.

Mahoney was completely confused. What was he talking about? "I don't know what to do with it!"

"Can you think of *nothing*?" he challenged her.

"I'm sure I could think of a million things to do with

Welcome to Mr. Magorium's Wonder Emporium . . .

. . . the most magical toy store in the world.

The eccentric Mr. Magorium ran the store . . .

. . . with the help of his assistant Mahoney.

A young boy named Eric spent almost every day there.

He was really good at building things . . . but he had a hard time making friends.

Henry, the store's accountant, had a hard time making friends, too.

One day Mr. Magorium announced he was leaving and wanted Mahoney to run the store.

The store threw a temper tantrum, and all the toys went haywire. Then it began turning gray.

Mahoney was afraid to run the store
and missed her old friend.

Eric and Henry knew she could do it,
they just had to convince her of it.

In the end she learned that believing in herself made all the magic happen.

it," she replied. "I could use it as a paperweight, use it to crush walnuts, dress it up for Christmas every year. I could —"

Mr. Magorium interrupted her. "Sure. There are thousands of useful things one might do with a block of wood, but what do you think might happen if just once someone believed in it?"

"Sir, I don't understand," Mahoney admitted. Mahoney and Mr. Magorium stared at one another. They had come to an awkward moment where neither of them knew what to say next.

Eric decided this would be the perfect time to discuss practical matters. He handed the brown paper bag to Mr. Magorium. "I brought you some stuff I thought you needed," he explained.

Mr. Magorium's face lit with delight. "Super!" he exclaimed happily.

Mahoney turned to Eric. "Listen, can you keep Mr. Magorium company while I speak with the doctor," she requested.

"Sure," Eric agreed as Mahoney walked out. He returned to the paper bag, taking out each item he'd brought. "Pj's . . . a toothbrush . . . a microscope. Here's a plank of wood," he continued, pulling the wood from his bag.

Mr. Magorium was delighted with the bag of treats. He stuck a hand in and pulled out an instrument that looked something like a large trumpet, and a bit like a tuba. "Eric?" he asked. "What is this?"

"It's a euphonium."

Mr. Magorium raised a questioning eyebrow. "They sell euphoniums in the gift shop?"

"No. I found it in the supply closet," Eric explained as he dragged a chair into the middle of the room and climbed on top of it. Once atop the chair, he busily set about affixing tiny glow-in-the-dark stars to every surface he could reach.

Mr. Magorium's face shone with happiness. He loved that Eric and Mahoney had come to visit him — and finding a euphonium in a hospital supply closet meant that the magic had followed him to the hospital. "Excellent!" he cried. He picked up the instrument and blew into it. *BARP!*

The blast brought Mahoney and a doctor scurrying into the room. "What on earth are you doing?" the doctor demanded to know.

"I'm practicing the euphonium," Mr. Magorium replied evenly, as though it were the most natural thing in the world.

“The what!?” the doctor asked.

“I thought I might give a concert in the psychiatric ward tomorrow,” Mr. Magorium informed him.

The doctor pulled the instrument from Mr. Magorium’s grasp. “There are people trying to sleep,” the doctor said angrily. “Where the heck did you even find this?”

“I found it in a supply closet,” Eric spoke up.

“We don’t keep musical instruments in our supply closet!” the doctor said.

“Well, where else would I have found it?” Eric asked, jumping down off the chair.

This was all too much for the doctor. “Okay . . . that’s it!” he exploded. He guided Eric and Mahoney toward the door. “You two — out of here! You can come back tomorrow.”

“Good-bye, Eric! Good-bye, Mahoney!” Mr. Magorium called, waving.

“Good-bye, sir,” Mahoney said. “Don’t leave before tomorrow.”

“Agreed,” Mr. Magorium said.

Mahoney and Eric waved as they exited the room, and the doctor shut the door behind them. “As for you,” he said to Mr. Magorium, “you need some rest.”

The doctor meanwhile began to move the chair that Eric had been standing on. "I wonder what that boy was doing on this chair?" he asked.

"Making sure I had enough space to sleep in," Mr. Magorium responded with a sly smile.

The doctor was confused, but it had been a strange day. He shook his head as he flipped off the lights and closed the door behind him. As the room descended into darkness it simultaneously exploded in a gleaming galaxy of glow-in-the-dark stars. Eric had adhered hundreds and hundreds of stickers to every possible surface in Mr. Magorium's room. There were stars on the ceiling, stars on the walls, and stars on the floor. There were even stars in Mr. Magorium's bed. The whole room was illuminated as if it held the entire cosmos. Magorium snuggled into his bed and smiled, feeling like he was floating somewhere very peaceful, deep in outer space.

CHAPTER TWELVE

That night Mahoney returned to her apartment feeling desperate. She plopped down on her couch and spoke to the Congreve Cube that sat on her coffee table. "All right, I need your help," she spoke to it. "Mr. Magorium is in the hospital right now. The store is a mess. The mutant is useless. Eric is worried. And I'm stuck." She sighed. That about summed it up. She had no idea what to do next.

She leaned closer to the cube. "If you're supposed to help me, please . . . do it now. Mr. Magorium can't leave. My time at the store can't end. I'm not ready." She hung her head. "Help me."

The cube sat on the table, looking as it always had — like a block of wood. "Maybe you can't help," she muttered, sitting back. "Maybe you're just a block of wood."

In the morning Mahoney went to get Mr. Magorium some fresh clothes but decided not to open the store for customers. Henry was waiting on a bench outside the store when she arrived. "Morning," he greeted her. "How's Mr. Magorium?"

"Fine," she answered stiffly. He wasn't exactly the person she wanted to see at that moment. He got up and followed her into the store.

The store was still gray and dreary but the mess had been cleaned. Mahoney figured that Bellini must have done it. He was always very reliable about keeping things in order.

"Is Mr. Magorium still . . . departing?" Henry asked.

"Not if I can help it," Mahoney said tensely.

"Good," Henry said. "I didn't know if you still needed me so I came in anyway."

"How long have you been waiting?" Mahoney asked,

"Not long. Just a couple of . . . hours. Are you keeping the store closed?"

She nodded as she headed toward the stairs to Mr. Magorium's apartment. The store remained quiet and gray as she passed by. "I just came to get Mr. Magorium fresh clothes," she said.

Henry shifted anxiously from foot to foot. "I'll . . . uh . . . "

Mahoney turned to look at Henry. What was wrong with him? Why was he acting so nervous?

"Do you mind if I work on the files?" he asked her.

Mahoney shrugged. What did it matter? "No. I suppose not," she said.

"Good. Thanks. Thank you," said Henry as he hurried to his office. He stopped short. "Unless . . . do you need me to work out here?"

Mahoney gazed around the quiet store. Normally the place was so busy; there would be a million things for him to do — even if it was closed. But today, the odd stillness was overwhelming.

Again, she wondered what was going on with Henry. Why was he so antsy?

Well, he wasn't her problem. He could do what he liked. She waved him away. "You can work wherever you want, Mutant. I don't care," she said.

"I mean, just in case there is an emergency," he explained, walking toward her. "Someone might need

something like . . . tiddlywinks or something. I could help them. It might be someone's birthday today, or someone might be a few blocks short or . . . whatever."

Mahoney gazed at him thoughtfully. It suddenly dawned on her; she realized what all this was about. "Do you want to run the store for the day?" she asked.

"Well, I'm here anyway —"

This was a side of him she had never seen. All he had ever cared about before were his precious books, and records, and files. But today — for some reason — he cared about what was happening in the store.

"Mutant," she cut him off sternly. If he wanted to run the store she expected him to be honest and say so. She stared at him and her expression said that she expected him to state exactly what he really meant.

"Okay," he gave in. "I want to run the store. This morning I waited in the cold on a very uncomfortable bench to offer to run the store."

Mahoney tilted her head questioningly. "Why?"

"Because I'm a jerk!" he blurted. "Last night, what I said about the insurance . . . it was something a jerk would say. I felt awful because I thought it might make you think I didn't care."

Mahoney nodded. He was right. It certainly had made her think he was an uncaring . . . jerk.

"It's just that other people bring flowers, send cards, give someone a hug or something," he went on. "I make sure everyone has their paperwork filled out properly. It's the only way I know to show I care. Today, though, I thought I'd try something different."

Mahoney thought of what Eric had told her. It's the only thing he knows how to talk about. How strange that a little boy had seen things more clearly than she had seen them. Maybe she had misjudged Henry.

Maybe he could help her — could even be a friend right now when she really needed a friend.

"Mutant, can I ask you something?" she said. "Do you think I have a sparkle?"

Henry scowled, confused. "Like glitter?"

"No. Like a sparkle." She struggled to explain what she meant. "Like something that reflects something big that's trying to get out." It sounded so silly. "Forget it. Never mind," she said, feeling foolish.

"You have a glint," Henry offered. "A twinkle. You have that thing you do with your fingers like you're playing an invisible piano."

"That's a quirk," she disagreed.

"A quirk's not a sparkle?" he asked.

"No."

He didn't get it. "Forget it, Mutant," she said. She

had wanted to know if he thought she had enough magic in her to run the store. It was crazy, though. Of course she didn't have magic! Mr. Magorium was magic. She was just . . . Mahoney.

But maybe there was still some way she could stop Mr. Magorium from departing. The beginning of an idea was forming inside her head.

She brought Mr. Magorium his fresh clothing and before long he was dressed and out of the hospital. He wore a sunny smile and his eyes looked rested. "So, Bluebell, shall we go to the store?" he suggested brightly.

"Actually, you're coming with me," she told him.

Mahoney led Mr. Magorium down the street. She checked every store window they passed until she came to a large discount mattress store. "Oooh, mattresses," Mr. Magorium said enthusiastically. "What a shame that I just woke up."

"Sir, you're going to have to follow my instructions," she told him. "I want you to follow me, do as I do — and then run out the door."

"Follow you, do as you do, run out the door," Mr. Magorium reviewed her instructions. "Perfect."

They went inside the mattress store. Mahoney had

never before seen Mr. Magorium look as confused as he did right then. But he waited patiently for her to take the lead.

After a brief search, she found what she had been looking for: a row of display beds that extended the entire length of the store. "I'm a little nervous about this," she quietly confided to Mr. Magorium.

"Why?" Mr. Magorium asked.

"It's mischievous and childish."

Mr. Magorium's eyes lit excitedly. "I can hardly wait!"

Mahoney called up all her nerve and readied herself for action. "All right," she instructed him in a whisper, "on GO."

Mr. Magorium frowned and shook his head. "Not on GO. It's always on GO."

"Okay," she agreed, thinking of a new signal, "on triskaidekaphobia."

Mr. Magorium shivered with giddy delight. "Oooh, that's a good one," he approved.

With one last deep inhale followed by a nervous exhale, she gave the signal. "Ready, set," she whispered. "Triskaidekaphobia!"

Mahoney set off running with Mr. Magorium right behind. At the very first bed, they jumped on, landing squarely in the middle. The springs in the mattress sent them bouncing off and onto the next bed — and the next, and the next! “This is splendid!” Mr. Magorium laughed.

From the corner of her eye, Mahoney noticed shocked customers watching them. A red-faced manager was rushing toward them. Still, she and Mr. Magorium continued bouncing from bed to bed.

After the last bed, Mahoney hit the floor running, heading for the front door. A quick check told her that Mr. Magorium was still right behind her. But so was the store’s angry manager!

They bounded out the front door, gasping with laughter and leaving the manager behind.

Their next stop was a very quiet clock store. It was packed with unusual, old clocks. The only sound was the gentle clicking of the clocks. But Mahoney had a plan to liven things up.

While Mahoney distracted the store manager by asking if he had a certain clock, Mr. Magorium set all the clocks to ring at the same moment. When he gave her the thumbs up, she left the store manager and joined him. “In forty-seven seconds,” he whispered, barely controlling his laughter. “This is terribly sweet of you, my dear.”

"I wanted you to see all the little things you'll miss if you leave," she told him seriously.

"I see," Mr. Magorium said. "I thought you were doing this to give me the best last day of anyone who ever lived."

Mahoney took hold of his arm. "This can't be your last day, sir," she pleaded.

"Ah, but it is," Mr. Magorium insisted in a kindly tone. "And now, thanks to you, it has been a remarkable one."

"No," Mahoney begged. She had been sure this plan of hers would work. She could see now that he was set on leaving.

"All I have left to do is use a public phone, wait in a line, and complain to a manager, and my life will be complete," he said.

"But, sir —"

"Shh," he interrupted. "It's almost time." He took her hand and gazed deeply into Mahoney's eyes.

All the chimes, bells, cuckoos, gongs, and alarms on the clocks all went off at once. Mr. Magorium's face shone with pure delighted happiness.

Mahoney's eyes welled with tears but she fought them down. She wasn't done yet.

CHAPTER THIRTEEN

That same morning, Eric put on his Mad Hatter top hat and went to the store. He arrived to find something he never would have expected in a million years. Henry was there all alone playing with some of the wooden dolls. The dolls had not come alive — none of the toys had — but Henry played with them just the same.

"Morning, Eric," Henry greeted him with a wooden doll in his hand that looked like the scientist Albert Einstein.

"Morning," Eric replied as he looked around at the gray, lifeless store. "Wow, it's quiet in here today."

"Yep," Henry agreed. "No one has come in. Mahoney left, so it's just been me thus far."

"You've been here all by yourself?" Eric asked, not quite believing that Henry would be willing or able to do such a thing.

"Yeah," Henry replied.

"And the store didn't collapse around you?"

Henry chuckled at this. "Nope."

Eric still couldn't make sense of it. It wasn't like Henry at all! "What are you doing?" he asked.

"Uh, taking down merchandise codes," he answered.

"No, I mean, what are doing with that doll?" Eric clarified.

"Oh, this?" he held up Einstein. "Nothing. I was just, you know, fiddling. Occupying time," Henry stammered.

"You mean, you were pretending?" Eric pressed.

"It's not pretending," Henry disagreed. "I was just doing this to keep my mind active while, you know, there wasn't much else to think about. Do you know what I mean?"

"Yeah," Eric said, nodding. "It's called pretending."

This news seemed to take Henry by surprise. He looked at the Einstein doll and then to Eric — and then back to the doll.

"It's okay, you can stay out here and play with the toys, Mutant," Eric told him. "I won't tell anyone."

The phone at the front counter rang and Eric picked it up. "Mr. Magorium's Wonder Emporium," he said in his most businesslike voice. The person on the other end sounded very familiar, but Eric couldn't make sense of what he was saying. He was asking if this was Magorium's Car Transmission Shop. "No, this is Mr. Magorium's Magic Emporium," he said.

"Good, then I'll bring my car right there," said the person on the other end of the phone. "Can you have it fixed by tonight?"

"Don't bring your car. We don't fix car transmissions!" Eric said again. What was wrong with this person?

The person laughed heartily. "Eric! It's me!"

Eric suddenly knew why the voice was familiar. "Mr. Magorium?" he asked.

"Yes! Yes!" Mr. Magorium answered happily. "You've just received the very first prank phone call I've ever made! And I'm calling from a public phone!" He sounded very excited about these facts, although Eric wasn't quite sure why it was so thrilling.

"Good for you, sir," Eric said.

"There are two things I must tell you," he went on. "Firstly: capital hat!"

Eric scrunched his forehead into a confused expression. How could Mr. Magorium possibly know?

"Secondly," Mr. Magorium continued. "I do wish you would make some friends."

Mr. Magorium asked to speak to Henry but the operator came on. "Please insert thirty-five more cents," she requested in her computerized voice.

"What?" Eric heard Mr. Magorium say on the other end of the line.

"Please insert thirty-five more cents," the operator said again.

"What?' Mr. Magorium repeated. Then he hung up the phone.

Eric looked over to Henry who was busy helping a little girl find a game she wanted. Whatever Mr. Magorium had wanted to tell Henry would have to wait until later.

A customer came to the register and Eric rang up the sale of a windup puppy. More and more customers arrived. Between them, Henry and Eric handled it all but they didn't have a moment to rest. Finally, around sunset, the last customers left. Henry locked the store door behind them. Turning toward Eric, he grinned. "Well, we handled ourselves pretty well," he said. "We make a good team."

"Yeah. I think so," Eric agreed. "There was no magic today though. Want to play checkers?"

Henry smiled, but the smile quickly faded. "No, I have to get back to the office."

"Come on, Henry," Eric pressed. "One game?"

Henry shook his head, "No. No. Some other time," he said as he walked away. As he headed to his office, he walked past the wall of stuffed animals, not noticing the same sock monkey puppet again reaching its arms out to him, as if trying to hug him.

Eric sighed. He was disappointed in Henry, but he decided not to give up on him. They had made a good team in the store earlier. Maybe he was someone who could be a friend. He decided he would wait for him to finish work in his office.

About an hour later, Henry was walking down the street away from the store to go home when Eric caught up with him. "Henry!" he shouted.

Henry seemed surprised to see Eric still there. "Hey, Eric. What are you doing here?"

"Well, um," Eric explained, "Mahoney usually walks me home, and it's getting kind of dark."

Henry sensed what he was getting at. "Do you want me to walk you home?" he asked.

Eric accepted his offer. "Thanks," he said.

They walked for half a block without talking before Henry spoke. "Eric, I have to ask, where do you get your hats?"

"From my room," Eric replied.

"Every day I see you in a different hat," Henry pointed out.

"Yeah. I collect them," Eric told him. "Mr. Magorium says I have the neatest hat collection he's ever seen."

"Really?" Henry was very interested. "I know people who own several hats, but I don't know if I've ever heard of a hat collection before."

"Would you like to see them?" Eric offered.

Henry agreed and walked Eric to his house. Upstairs, on one of the walls in Eric's room, hung rows and rows of different hats — a hard hat, different baseball caps, hats for different jobs, hats worn by a variety of characters from books, hats from around the world. They were neatly organized, and sparkly strands of lights were twisted between them. "Pretty neat, huh?" Eric said proudly.

Henry agreed that they were neat and even tried on a jester's cap before leaving. Eric was glad he had gotten to know Henry better. But as he sat on his bed, he was once again worried. What was happening with Mr. Magorium?

CHAPTER FOURTEEN

Mr. Magorium and Mahoney stopped at an ice cream vendor's cart and bought themselves each an ice cream cone. Everything was going just as Mahoney had hoped it would.

As they licked their scoops of ice cream, they headed into the park. In her arms, Mahoney held a roll of bubble wrap, the kind they used at the store to ship toys and other breakable things. She stopped when they came to a flat, cemented part of the park near a water fountain. "Here is good, sir," she said.

She gave Mr. Magorium her cone to hold and then

unfurled the twelve-foot-long roll of bubble wrap, throwing it down on the cement as though it were a magic carpet. Stepping back, she took Mr. Magorium's cone and her own back from him.

"Now what?" Mr. Magorium asked her.

Mahoney smiled at him. "Well . . . we dance," she said.

Mr. Magorium grinned broadly as he realized what she had in mind. He hopped onto the bubble wrap and began doing a lively jig. The bubble wrap snapped and popped beneath his feet. With each loud snap, Mr. Magorium laughed harder and harder. "This is brilliant!" he shouted, still dancing his jubilant jig. "Wait! Wait!"

He jumped higher and faster!

POP!

SNAP!

POP! POP! POP!

"Delightful!" he cried gleefully. He reached out for Mahoney, pulling her onto the bubble wrap to dance with him.

But something strange happened.

No matter where Mahoney stepped, she couldn't get the bubble wrap to pop.

Mahoney and Mr. Magorium stopped dancing. They stared down at the bubble wrap, trying to figure out why this was happening. "That's odd," Mr. Magorium murmured.

Mahoney stepped off the bubble wrap. What had just happened proved her point. She was so not-magic that bubble wrap wouldn't even pop for her!

She decided it was a good time for them to talk about the store. "Sir . . ." she began.

"Yes dear?" Mr. Magorium said, still studying the bubble wrap, trying to figure out why it wouldn't pop for Mahoney.

"I think we need to have a talk," Mahoney said.

Mr. Magorium looked up at her, forgetting the bubble wrap. "Oooh, what shall we discuss?" he asked, sounding enthused at the prospect of an interesting discussion. "Wait! I have a good topic. Black gumdrops: why?"

"No, sir. I want to discuss the Emporium," she told him.

"Of course," he agreed. "I think you'll do a fantastic job with it."

"Sir, I can't run it!" she insisted.

"Nonsense!" he cried.

"I can't. And if you're leaving so I'm forced to — I'm afraid I might fail you," she said.

"Never," Mr. Magorium disagreed. "You are a young woman of great potential."

"That's it, Mr. Magorium. I might have potential but that's it. All I have is potential — nothing more than that," she told him.

"When I was a little girl I was gifted at playing the piano. I could play Rachmaninoff's Second Piano Concerto and I remember everyone talking about my potential. And at ten, I played Rachmaninoff's Second. At fifteen — Rachmaninoff's Second."

She studied Mr. Magorium's kindly face. Did he understand what she was trying to tell him?

"I'm twenty-five," she continued, "and you're still telling me about my potential. If someone asks me to play the song I know the best . . . I play Rachmaninoff's Second."

Mr. Magorium gazed at her intently. She could see he was thinking about what she'd just said. She was eager to hear what wise thing he'd say next. "It's a very good piece, Rachmaninoff's Second," he said at last. "I knew Rachmaninoff. We were doubles partners in tennis. And I love his Second Piano Concerto."

Mahoney's eyes widened with exasperation. He hadn't understood what she'd meant at all!

"But I concur that you must play something else," he added.

Mahoney relaxed a bit. Maybe he had understood

after all. He took hold of her hand. "Might I suggest that you play Molly Mahoney's First," he said as he reached to hold her hand. "I agree that you must go forward," he continued. "Now let us go forward with the rest of our day."

Mahoney sighed and nodded. She did have a few more things in mind. They played games and flew a kite on a beach near the park.

At suppertime, they lined up to buy hotdogs from a vendor's truck near the beach. As they moved up on the line, Mr. Magorium grew more and more excited. He was planning to do yet another thing he'd never done before — complain to a manager.

When they were at the front of the line, Mr. Magorium spoke to the teenage boy behind the counter in a stern voice as if he wanted to complain about something. "May I speak with your manager?" he asked.

The young man turned to another teenager in the truck. "Tim? This guy wants to speak to you," he told him.

Mr. Magorium turned to Mahoney and winked. He looked like a child about to pull a great prank. She loved seeing him so excited and happy.

"May I help you?" Tim the manager asked Mr. Magorium.

“Are you the manager of this hotdog truck?” Mr. Magorium asked, pretending to be angry.

“Uh . . . yeah,” Tim answered.

Mr. Magorium stared at him for a moment and then reached up to shake his hand. “It’s an absolute honor to meet you,” he said as he shook. “I was going to complain but I’m just . . . I’m simply too moved.”

“Cool,” Tim replied, staring at Mr. Magorium as though he were a lunatic.

Mahoney smiled and shook her head in amusement as she ordered their hotdogs. Who else but Mr. Magorium could find such pleasure in meeting the manager of a hotdog truck? There was no one else like him.

As they ate their hotdogs, Mahoney and Mr. Magorium walked along the boardwalk near the beach. Mr. Magorium pulled a paper from his jacket pocket. “What is this?” Mahoney asked.

“That’s a handbill of me in eighteen-twenty-four when I was living in Switzerland,” he said, handing it to her. On it was a drawing of Mr. Magorium smiling pleasantly and sitting behind a table at a carnival. On the front of the table was a sign that read: THE MIRACLE OF FLIGHT. “That was the first amusement I ever sold,” he explained, “the very, very, very first creased contraption of gossamer aviation.”

Mahoney studied the handbill more closely. On the table sat a single paper airplane. "It's a paper airplane," she remarked.

"All right, sure," he admitted, "if you want to ruin a name like 'creased contraption of gossamer aviation.'"

"How amazing," Mahoney said quietly. Mr. Magorium was the person who had invented the paper airplane. She could hardly believe it.

"I sold it for five francs," he went on. "Unfortunately, I only made one and the advertising cost me ten francs." He stopped walking a moment and shook his head at his own foolishness. "What can I say? I live in the abstract."

"What did you do after you sold it?" Mahoney asked.

"I built another one and sold it," he recalled. "But, this time, instead of selling it to Mr. Hikkenloger, I sold it to the prince. Soon I was manufacturing toys for the Royal Family and, after a while, I saved enough money to come to the States and open a small store."

"The Wonder Emporium?" Mahoney guessed.

"Indeed," he replied. He stopped and faced Mahoney. "You see, everyone is given the opportunity for a remarkable life, Mahoney, including you. I have lived mine and now I am moving on. You must live your life now

and conduct it however you think is right. You must be brave and thoughtful and conduct it with all your might. It is the only life you have."

Mahoney did not like his serious tone. It seemed like something important was about to happen — as though these were his final words to her. She wanted to turn away, but she forced herself to listen carefully instead. If Mr. Magorium had something important to tell her, she didn't want to miss it.

"Why else would all this beauty and inspiration and hope be put here if not for something great?" he continued. "Your life may not be exactly what you expected but, I would argue, it may be something even more than you expected. Your life is an occasion, Mahoney! Rise to it!"

As he finished speaking, fireworks exploded back by the hotdog stand. The night sky was alight with spectacular lights fizzing and zooming all around.

Once the fireworks ended, they headed over to the Emporium. Inside the store, Mr. Magorium switched on a few lights, just enough for them to see their way through the maze of toys. They entered the store bubbling over with laughter, still feeling jubilant from all the fun they had earlier in the day.

However, once their laughter subsided, a silence settled over them like a dark, heavy blanket. They stood looking at one another for what felt like an eternity. Then suddenly and with a fury, Mahoney leaped up and grabbed Mr. Magorium in a fierce squeeze, desperate to keep him there.

"Mahoney," Mr. Magorium said soothingly.

"Don't go," Mahoney pleaded with him as they stood together embracing in the middle of the store. "Stay one more day."

"I can't," he said sadly and yet matter-of-factly.

"Please," she begged, the tears forming in the corners of her eyes. "Just not tonight. Not right now. Just give me a little longer. I'm not ready for it to end."

Mr. Magorium extended his arms away from Mahoney and looked at her lovingly. He sighed deeply, paused, and started to explain, of all things, Shakespeare. "When King Lear dies in Act Five," he began, "do you know what Shakespeare wrote?"

Mahoney looked at him, confused.

"'He dies,'" Mr. Magorium continued. "That's all — and nothing more. No fanfare, no metaphor, no brilliant final words. The culmination of the most influential work of dramatic literature is, 'He dies.'"

Mahoney tried to follow.

"And yet," he went on, "every time I read those two words I find myself overcome with melancholy. But not because of the words, but because of the life that came before those words . . . . I've lived all five of my acts, Mahoney."

Mahoney sniffed a bit as tears streamed down her cheeks.

"I am not asking you to be happy that I must go," Magorium implored knowingly, "I am only asking that you turn the page, continue reading, and let the next story begin. And if anyone ever asks what became of me, you relate my life in all its wonder, and say simply and modestly, 'He died.'"

"I'm going to miss you so much," Mahoney cried before being wrapped into a warm hug. "I love you," she whispered.

"I love you, too," he replied.

"Is there anything I can do?" she asked.

"Find your life," Mr. Magorium said gently.

As they held one another, Mr. Magorium tried his hardest not to cry. Then he said, "I am so proud of you."

Mahoney was confused. "Why? I haven't done anything yet."

"But you will," said Mr. Magorium with a smile full of promise and belief.

And with one last hug, Mahoney turned and headed for the door. Once she was outside, she looked back through the window for one final bittersweet wave good-bye.

Mr. Magorium waited until Mahoney was gone, and then he picked up a paper airplane and sent it soaring through the store. He was happy to see that, this time, the plane did not drop to his feet. It seemed to sense what he was about to say and was rising above its sorrow to give him this last flight.

He sat on the piano bench and spoke to the store. His voice was firm, like that of a loving but concerned parent. "I had hoped you would improve by now," he said to the gray, quiet store. "It breaks my heart to leave you like this. You must hold on. You must! She will find it. She will give you all that you need."

His head swiveled as he followed the plane's progress around the store. Then he turned his attention back to the store and spoke some more. "You have been my greatest achievement, my shining glory, and now my legacy. I do so hope that you end this

despair and return once again to all that is good in the world."

He stood, turning in every direction, taking in every inch of his beloved store. "I hate to leave you, but I cannot stay," he told the store lovingly. "Good-bye."

The paper airplane came to rest at his feet. And there it remained.

CHAPTER FIFTEEN

Mr. Magorium's funeral took place on a rainy day. Despite the weather, many, many people came out to say good-bye and show respect for the man who had brought so much fun and laughter into their lives.

And even though the day was dreary, it was not as bleak as the store. Every color in the Emporium had faded into gray: the wood, the toys, the mobiles, and every wall. Large portions of the store sat in complete darkness. Not a single toy moved.

Even Mahoney could not bring the store to life. The windup and electric toys that once sprang into action

when she passed now sat listlessly, barely noticing her as she walked by. When she turned on the register, the cash drawer slid open noiselessly.

Everyone felt the sadness. Bellini came up from the basement but he could only manage to sit in the book balcony, holding his head mournfully in his large hands.

Eric gazed for awhile at the gray stuffed animals and then joined Mahoney at the register. "It's not that bad," he said hopefully. "We can bring it back, right Mahoney?"

But Mahoney didn't answer him. She simply stood at the register gazing blankly around her.

"Mahoney?" Eric prodded, but still got no reply. He sighed. Was she just giving up? He couldn't let that happen! "Let's just run the store and see if it picks up," he suggested.

Mahoney turned to him as she headed for the door. "I'm sorry, Eric," she said.

Eric ran after her. "I'll help you — just don't leave!" he pleaded.

She stopped by the door and spoke to him. "I'm sorry. I can't."

"It just needs a little magic," he said.

"I know," she agreed, "but I don't have any."

* * *

As Mahoney rode the bus home that day, she had the unfamiliar sensation that she was just like everyone else on the bus. Before this day she had always felt out of place. Now, for the first time ever, she felt as though she fit in, that she was average and normal. She had always imagined that this would be a good feeling. But she wasn't quite sure that she liked it.

Perhaps it was that she was still so sad about Mr. Magorium leaving. Maybe, in time, she would grow to enjoy being average.

When she got home she sat in her apartment gazing at the Congreve Cube for a long while. It just sat there. Why had she ever, even for a moment, believed it could help her?

Anything had seemed possible while Mr. Magorium was around. But now he was gone.

Mahoney began to cry. It felt good, in a way, to let all the grief and loss inside her heart spill out. She cried for a long, long time.

Two days later, on the other side of town, Henry sat at his desk in a cramped cubicle at the accounting firm where he worked. He got up to go get a drink from the water fountain and was barraged by his co-workers. They kept stopping him, giving him forms to file and accounts to review. By the time he was at the end of the hallway, his arms were piled high with papers. It was the very same thing he had done nearly every day before Mr. Magorium hired him — and it was depressing.

He passed the office of his boss, Ms. Fludd. She called to him, "Henry, did you finish that clearing house account like I asked you?"

He peered at her over his tower of papers and blinked. "You asked me to finish a clearing house account?" It wasn't like him to forget something Ms. Fludd asked him to do.

"Last Tuesday," she said sternly. "I need it by tomorrow."

"But I haven't . . . you didn't," he sputtered.

"Tomorrow, Henry," she insisted, returning to the work on her desk.

When Henry got back to his cubicle, he found Mahoney sitting there. "Hi," he said as he squeezed around her to get to the other side of his desk.

"Hey," she replied.

He settled his pile of papers onto the desk. "So, how are you?"

“Really, really sad,” she admitted.

“Yeah, I’m . . . I’m sorry,” he said. “But, you’ll be happy to know that store is in good shape financially. It has a very stable profitability.”

“Great . . . that’s great,” she muttered, though it didn’t seem to Henry that she was all that interested.

“But I went by yesterday and I noticed it was closed,” he added.

“Yeah,” she said dully, nodding.

He took a deep breath. He didn’t want to say anything to upset her but he had to say something. “Molly, I realize it may be a little hard for you right now,” he began, “but are you planning on letting it stay closed?”

“I don’t know what else to do,” she told him.

“Well, from a financial point of view, every day that store stays closed it’s losing value. It’s my professional opinion that, if you’re going to keep it, you should keep it open. You have to run it in order to make a profit.”

Mahoney looked at him, her expression completely miserable. “I can’t! Not on my own.”

He knew this was how she felt, so her words didn’t surprise him. He’d already given the situation some thought. “Well, okay . . . then the only solution would be to sell it. I can put it on the market as soon as tomorrow morning, if you’d like.”

Mahoney stared at him but she didn't say anything. He couldn't read her expression, either. "Mahoney?" he checked.

She continued to stare.

"Do you want me to, uh, call a real estate agent?" he pressed her for an answer.

Tears filled Mahoney's eyes and quickly spilled over. They kept coming, faster and heavier by the second.

Henry had never been able to stand seeing anyone cry. He found it extremely unsettling. "Oh, oh, okay, okay," he stammered, getting to his feet with no idea how to handle the situation. "Oh, boy . . . okay."

He felt he should try to comfort her so he wrapped his arm around her. She leaned her head on his shoulder and let her tears flow freely. "Okay, okay," he said soothingly.

CHAPTER SIXTEEN

Eric woke up and found himself wanting to wear an average sort of hat. Like Mahoney, he had also been feeling more average than ever before in his life since Mr. Magorium had departed.

He picked the most regular, normal hat from his closet, a soft, blue cloth hat with a brim all around, the kind fishermen often wore. Putting it on, he went down to the store to see how things were going. It had been several days since Mahoney had locked the doors after Mr. Magorium's funeral. He hoped she'd finally gotten around to reopening it.

When Eric got there, though, the store was still closed and there was a sign in the window that read: FOR SALE. Peering through the front window, he saw that the store was still in its sad, gloomy state.

He couldn't just leave it like that! He had to find Mahoney, get her to open up the store, and take down the awful sign.

Eric decided to head for Mahoney's apartment. He didn't know exactly where it was but he knew what bus she took and that it took her only fifteen minutes to get to the store. If he rode the bus for fifteen minutes, it should bring him to her neighborhood.

But as he waited for the bus, he noticed a sign in front of a hotel across the street: COME HEAR MOLLY MAHONEY ON THE PIANO.

Hurrying across, he went into the lounge. A piano played softly in the lobby. He approached her directly, interrupting her song. "What are you doing?" he demanded to know.

"Eric?" Molly said, surprised to see him there.

"What are you doing?" he asked again.

"I'm playing a song. It's called 'Jennifer Juniper,'" she told him.

"Why?" he asked.

"Someone requested it," she replied.

"No," Eric said, shaking his head. "Why are you here? Why are you doing this?"

"I have to make money," she explained.

"Then run the store," he said.

Mahoney frowned. "I can't."

"Is that why it's for sale?" Eric insisted on knowing.

Mahoney gazed down unhappily. "Yeah," she said quietly in a sad tone. "I'm sorry, Eric," she added. "I don't want to let you down."

Eric looked around at the fancy hotel. People rushed through the lobby. No one was paying attention to Mahoney's music. He didn't notice anyone having fun. "Is this what *you* want?" he asked her.

"No," she admitted. "But I can't do anything else."

He was tired of the way she was acting. "Stop *saying* that!" he shouted.

"Eric, I know this hard on you," she said. "It's hard on me, too. But I can't be a kid anymore!"

"I know," he said.

"You do?"

"Yeah, I do," he told her. He knew because he'd heard her say it so often lately. "You have to start the rest of your life!"

"Exactly!" she said.

"But the rest of your life is at the store!" he insisted.

She stared at him with a shocked expression.

He waited for her to say something. Did she understand what he was saying? He wasn't sure. If Mr. Magorium hadn't been able to convince her, how could he hope to? It was probably useless for him to try anymore. Hanging his head, he trudged out of the hotel lobby.

As he came out onto the sidewalk, a bus was pulling up to the stop. It wasn't Mahoney's bus. It was the bus he'd seen Henry take. Henry had told him where he worked and Eric was pretty sure that this bus would take him to Henry's office.

Checking that the way was clear, Eric bolted across the street. But he didn't get on the bus. Instead, he began to run home. He had a sudden idea, one that might save the store. If his plan was going to work, though, there were a few things he had to do first.

CHAPTER SEVENTEEN

After she finished playing piano at the hotel, Mahoney walked down the block and opened the store, but not because she meant to run it. She was meeting a real estate agent who had noticed the FOR SALE sign and called her cell phone while she was at the hotel. He'd told her his name was Barry and that he wanted to bring a woman named Mrs. Arroyo and her son, Jack, to see the store. Mrs. Arroyo was interested in buying it.

Mahoney sat behind the counter and poked at the Congreve Cube, which she had brought back to the store the day before. But it just sat there, quiet and ordinary as ever.

Mahoney gazed around the store, frowning. It certainly wasn't looking its best.

It wasn't long before the real estate agent arrived with his client and her son. It was easy to tell that Mrs. Arroyo was a business woman who meant business. She wore a gray, striped suit, serious glasses, and had her hair pulled back off her frowning face.

Mahoney looked down at Jack. She thought he seemed like a nice boy, but way too serious for someone so young.

With them, was Barry, a man in a mustard-yellow jacket that all salesmen from his agency wore. "You will notice the original woodwork is still here," he told Mrs. Arroyo as they came into the store.

Mrs. Arroyo wrinkled her nose in disgust. "Well, we can rip that out," she said.

"It comes fully stocked with toys," he added.

"No wonder this store is going out of business," she said. "Does anyone even play with old toys like these anymore?"

"Sure they do," Mahoney said, walking toward them. She noticed Jack looking up at a toy on a shelf. It was a gyro-wheel, a handheld toy with two parallel tracks and a metal wheel.

Like the other toys in the store, the gyro-wheel lay

quietly on its side, gray and sad looking. "Can I play with that?" he asked, pointing to the toy.

"Don't touch anything, Jack," Mrs. Arroyo snapped at her son.

"It's fine, ma'am," Mahoney assured her, "he can play with anything he likes." She reached up and got the gyro-wheel for Jack. He turned it around in his hands, looking confused. "Do you know how it works?" Mahoney asked him.

He shook his head. "I have no idea."

"Okay. I'll show you," she said as she picked the gyro-wheel up in her hand. She began to tilt it back and forth. Soon, the circular wheel of the toy began turning. Then, as if on its own accord, the wheel began its journey back and forth on the curved metal tracks.

"Wow! That's neat!" Jack cried, delighted.

"It's a magnet," Mahoney explained.

"How does the magnet work?" Jack asked.

"I don't know," Mahoney admitted.

"Is it magic?"

Mahoney had to think about that one. It seemed to her that science was a way of explaining the magic in the world. Some scientist, like a very clever student of magic, had figured out how nature worked this particular trick.

But it was magic, just the same. “I believe it is,” she told Jack.

Mahoney smiled as Jack walked away; he was completely enamored with the simple toy. However her smile soon faded when she had to return to Barry and Mrs. Arroyo, who had opened the Door of Rooms. It showed them only the staircase, as it had since it turned gray. “I have to say, the use of this space is completely impractical,” Mrs. Arroyo told Mahoney.

“It wasn’t designed to be practical,” Mahoney replied.

Mrs. Arroyo gave a disgusted snort and walked off into the back of the store. “Well, it’s certainly a large enough space for the price, although everything would have to be gutted and redone,” she said as though talking to herself. She turned back to Mahoney. “Are you willing to come down on the price if I pay in cash?”

“I guess so,” Mahoney agreed uncertainly.

“Well, if I take it I’d have to start knocking down walls right away.” Her eyes flickered across the store, taking it all in. “Are the fixtures included?” she asked.

“Entirely,” Barry said eagerly.

Mrs. Arroyo nodded as she strolled toward the front counter. She picked up the Congreve Cube. “What’s

this?" Mahoney told her it was the Congreve Cube and that it, too, came with the store. "Does it do anything?" Mrs. Arroyo asked.

"I don't know," Mahoney replied.

Mrs. Arroyo stared at Mahoney as though she though Mahoney must be a real fool. "Great. Okay," she sneered. "I'll let you know what I decide." She searched around for her son. "Come on, Jack, we're leaving," she called.

Jack came running out from behind a shelf. His face no longer wore the serious scowl he'd come in with. Now he was smiling happily. "It's magic. The gyro thing is magic!"

Mrs. Arroyo took his hand and hurried him toward the front door. "Come on, we have other properties to look at."

Barry, the real estate man, hurried after them. "We'll be in touch," he told Mahoney quickly.

"Thanks," she murmured. Sighing deeply, she noticed that they'd left open the Door of Rooms. As she went back to close it, she walked past the gyro-wheel lying on its side on a shelf, not noticing that all its original bright, cheerful color had returned to it. In the bleak, gray store, it stood out like a brilliant flower on a rainy day.

CHAPTER EIGHTEEN

eanwhile, Eric had arrived at Henry's office and asked to be directed to his tiny cubicle.

He had put on his only suit, a blue tie, and he wore his best black bowler hat. He needed to look like a serious business man if Henry was going to believe a word he planned to say.

Henry sat at his desk punching numbers into his calculator and writing the results on a large ledger sheet. Eric stood in the cubicle doorway and coughed lightly to get his attention.

Henry looked up sharply. "Eric?"

Eric strode into the cubicle and stood before Henry.

He made his voice as businesslike and grown-up as he could manage. "I am here to make you a substantial offer for the store," he stated.

Henry's brow creased with confusion. "What?"

"I realize that I am only a kid and that I can't offer you the full price for the store," he went on. "But I think you might be interested in what I have to offer."

A small smile formed on Henry's lips. Eric could tell that Henry did not think he was serious.

Eric had thought this through, though. His offer made perfect sense — at least to him it did.

"Hear me out," Eric continued. "I am prepared to offer Mahoney a down payment of two-hundred-and-thirty-seven dollars in pennies, nickels, dimes, and a Christmas check from my grandma."

He had calculated his money on the bus ride over. "After that," he went on, "I am willing to pay you my allowance and a hefty percentage of the store's profits on a weekly basis. Keep in mind, that my young age works as a *benefit* as it means that I have more weeks left in my life than the typical buyer, which means more *allowances*."

Eric folded his arms, satisfied that he had made a strong argument for why Mr. Magorium's Wonder

Emporium should be sold to him and that his offer was impossible to refuse.

Henry sighed deeply. "Why are you doing this?" he asked Eric.

Eric thought of a lot of things he could say. He might tell Henry that he had always wanted to invest in a building. He could say he thought it was a smart way to make money, a good business deal. He even thought of claiming that he wanted to make his mark on the city.

In the end, though, he didn't want to lie to Henry. "I don't want someone else to have the store!" he blurted. "All right? I don't want it to change!"

He suddenly felt that he *had* to have the store, no matter what it took to get it. "I'll even throw in my hat collection!" he offered.

Henry came around from behind his desk. He sat beside Eric. "Don't throw in your hat collection," he advised in a kind voice.

Henry didn't understand how much this meant to him. "There has to be something I can do," he pleaded. "Please! Mahoney is about to make a terrible mistake and we have to stop her. If she sells that store, any chance she has of ever figuring out how special she is will be gone! We can't let her do that! Please, as my friend, help me!"

"There must be something we can figure out," Henry said in a thoughtful voice.

Eric looked at him hopefully. Henry was smart. If anyone could figure out a way to save the store, he could. But would he be able to think of a plan in time?

CHAPTER NINETEEN

Mahoney sat playing with the gyro-wheel until after dark. She'd locked up the store but couldn't bear to leave. She felt like crying and so she did, letting the tears fall freely down her cheeks.

After crying a while, she heard a rapping from the front window. Standing and wiping her eyes, she saw Henry standing outside. She opened the door for him. "What are you doing here?" she asked as he stepped in.

"I have good news," he told her. "You have an offer on the store. A good offer. A cash offer. If you look it over tonight, you can sign the papers and the deal can be done by tomorrow."

Mahoney stared at the papers and back to Henry. "Do you think I should take it?" she asked him.

"I think it's a good offer," he replied.

"But do you think I should take it?" she asked again. He hadn't exactly answered her question the first time.

"I think it will make things easier," he said.

Mahoney was becoming irritated with him. Why wouldn't he answer her question? "But do you think I should take it?" she asked a third time, her voice rising impatiently.

"Answering as an accountant, yes," he said. "I think this kind of offer is more than we expected. It's one of a kind, and you'd be foolish not to take it. But I'm not here as an accountant. I'm speaking now as your friend and I don't believe anyone can offer what this store is truly worth to you."

What she was she hearing from him? He had to be joking! "You don't even believe in this store, Mutant," she scoffed.

"No," he replied. "But I believe in you."

She didn't want to hear this. "Unfortunately, I'm not much to believe in," she said, walking away from him and toward the front counter. "Mr. Magorium could make the wildest, most amazing things happen with a

flick of his wrist, a bat of his eye: I can't even finish what I start!"

Henry followed her. The two of them sat behind the counter for a moment without speaking until Henry noticed the Congreve Cube. "What's the block?" he asked.

"Oh . . . it's the Congreve Cube. It's supposed to help me unlock some great mystery or something," Mahoney replied.

He leaned toward the cube on the counter and studied it. "It's just a block of wood," he commented.

"There's that word . . . *just*," she snapped at him.

"It is," he insisted. "It's *just* a block of wood."

"A magical block of wood, Mutant," she said, feeling more impatient with him than ever before. "It's a block of wood that, probably, in the right hands, could reveal some greatness we can't even imagine!"

Henry shook his head, not believing it. "Sorry. That's impossible."

Mahoney wanted to shake him. How could he be so thickheaded? "How could you have missed it?" she cried. "Every minute, every day, in every corner of the store — impossible things were happening!"

"Do you honestly believe that?" Henry questioned doubtfully.

"Yes!"

"You believe that this store was magic?" he checked.

"You just never saw it," she told him.

"And you believe that this block of wood is really more than a block of wood?" he asked.

Mahoney turned away from him and took several steps into the store. "Absolutely!" she answered. "I believe it with my entire heart!"

A second after she spoke those words, the Congreve Cube — all by itself — turned over onto its side!

Henry's eyes went wide with amazement. How had it done that?

Mahoney kept on talking. She hadn't seen what the cube had done because she was facing the other way. "The sad truth is that only Mr. Magorium could make the store show its magic. It was his Emporium, not mine. They were his blocks, his toys, and his magic." She sighed in defeat. "Thank you for coming, but it's over."

Henry continued to stare with astonishment at the Congreve Cube. Had he really seen what he thought he'd seen?

He needed to test it once again. "Tell me one more time that it's more than a block of wood," he said.

"It's absolutely more than a block of wood," Mahoney said firmly, turning back toward him.

She was in time to see the Congreve Cube flip onto its side yet again.

Mahoney gasped. "What? What's making it move?"

"I have no idea," Henry replied, not taking his eyes off the cube.

As Mahoney walked slowly toward the cube, she remembered what Mr. Magorium had said to her: *There are thousands of useful things one might do with a block of wood; but what do you think might happen if just once someone believed in it?*

Mahoney came alongside the cube and put her face down next to it. "Move," she whispered.

The Congreve Cube rolled four times. It only stopped because it had rolled up against the cash register and could go no further.

Mahoney and Henry exchanged a darting glance. "Don't worry," she told the cube. "If you fall, I'll just pick you right back up." She shut her eyes, trying hard to stay in touch with how much she believed in the Congreve Cube. "Move," she said.

The Congreve Cube started to roll once again. It moved around the cash register, picking up speed as it went.

The cash register began to turn back to its former color.

The cube raced around the counter, going faster and faster. Soon it was skidding around corners, zooming over every inch of the counter. And wherever it touched — color sprang up in its wake.

The cube was going so fast it was almost a blur. It flew up into the air, spinning so quickly it looked round. It sped around the store like lightning, bringing back the colors of the Emporium wherever it touched!

Mahoney realized what had brought out the magic in the cube. She had said she believed in it, truly believed with all her heart — just as Mr. Magorium had told her!

It was also what the store had wanted. It couldn't be magic for someone who didn't believe in it or in herself!

Mahoney was so excited she could barely catch her breath.

She glanced at Henry to see how he was reacting. He was pale and goggle-eyed with amazement.

The cube suddenly changed direction in midair! It scorched a path toward him, going at top speed. Henry sputtered, trying to say something to her. But as the cube neared him, he fainted onto the floor.

Mahoney rushed to help him but noticed something strange. It was still gray on the floor underneath Henry.

Glancing around, she saw that, although much of the store had returned to its former glory, patches of it were still gray.

All at once she understood what still had to be done. The cube and the store needed to know if Henry believed in it. He had gotten her to say she believed in the store, even though she hadn't entirely realized it herself.

Now she had to find a way to get him to say it. Would he admit that he believed or would his sensible side win out in the end?

CHAPTER TWENTY

Henry stayed asleep on the floor until early the next morning. He awoke to find Mahoney looking down at him. "Morning, Mutant," she greeted him cheerily.

Henry sat up slowly. He rubbed his head. "I must have hit my head when I passed out," he said, wincing with pain.

"I didn't see you pass out," Mahoney said.

"Yes, you did, last night," he reminded her.

Mahoney shook her head. "Last night I went home." She looked away from him. She hated fooling him like this but she had a plan in mind, a plan to make him realize that he also believed in magic.

"The Congreve Cube, it flew around the room," he insisted.

"Mutant, I think you must have dreamt that," she said. "I left you here to finalize the paperwork for the sale of the store. You must have fallen asleep."

"No, I didn't!" Henry disagreed urgently. "I passed out after I saw that cube fly."

"Cubes can't fly," Mahoney said with a small smile that she hid from Henry by turning her head.

"Of course they can," Henry said.

From the corner of her eye, she saw an entire group of toys return to their original bright splendor. It was working!

"Well, it doesn't matter now," she went on. "I'm selling the store."

"What?!" Henry gasped, getting to his feet.

"Remember the offer?" she asked him. "We're signing the deal this morning."

"You . . . you c-can't!" he sputtered.

She walked away from him and he trailed after her. "Why can't I?" she asked.

"Because it's . . . it's magic!" he cried.

Another group of toys regained their color.

"Isn't that a little difficult to believe?" Mahoney asked, again hiding her smile.

"No," he disagreed. "Not anymore. I believe it almost completely."

More of the store shone brightly!

"The cube — it flew all round the store," he continued. "It's you! You're the block of wood. You just have to believe."

Mahoney stopped and froze. That was it! He was right! Why hadn't she realized it sooner? "I'm a block of wood," she repeated, turning around to face Henry. "And, apparently, a block of wood can do anything."

She felt an odd sensation rise up inside of her. Was it a twinkle — a glint?

"Holy cow!" Henry gasped.

"What is it?" she asked, alarmed.

"I see it in your eyes. It's a sparkle!" he told her.

Mr. Magorium had told her she had a sparkle — and here it was, at last! It was the magic he had always said she had inside.

Mahoney moved her hand and the toy piano played a chord. She stopped moving . . . and the piano stopped.

Mahoney waved her hands through the air like a conductor. The piano played with all its heart. Soon she was leading it in playing the song she had tried so hard to complete, but this time she didn't pause or fumble;

she blew right past the part that had always tripped her up before.

As Mahoney and the piano played more brilliantly than either of them had ever played before, the store came fully to life. Not one speck of gray remained!

The magnets in the science section levitated. The kites once again ruffled in a wind only they could feel. The windup and remote-control toys moved, all on their own. The mobiles all began to spin.

Bellini came up from the basement. He saw what was happening and grinned — wider than anyone had ever seen him smile.

With every note, Mahoney felt more joyful and sure of herself. With every movement of her arms, the store was brought back to its original, shining, lovely, active, and magical self.

Henry watched all this from the stuffed animal wall. He jumped with a startle as he felt something brush against his arm and was surprised to see it was the sock monkey puppet, reaching out at him. As the monkey rested its head on his shoulder, Henry relaxed, smiled, and hugged him back.

In the next second, a stuffed ostrich curled his long neck around his arm. A fat, fluffy elephant wrapped him in a hug with its trunk. Soon all the stuffed animals reached out to hug him, and Henry hugged each of them in return.

Mahoney came over and put her arms around Henry in a warm squeeze. Henry was the one who had helped her find the magic within herself. By believing in her he'd helped her believe in herself, and the magic of the store. She felt truly grateful for him.

Then Eric approached Mahoney and Eric, and hugged them both. More and more customers walked over to the wall to be a part of the collective embrace. Before long, everyone in the store was enveloped in a giant group hug made up of stuffed animals, toys, and people.

In the center of the group, Mahoney and Henry were face to face. "I know you hate this word," he said to her, "but I have to tell you that you're just amazing!"

This time she didn't mind the way it sounded and she smiled brighltly at him.

CHAPTER TWENTY-ONE

So, Molly Mahoney ran Mr. Magorium's Wonder Emporium after all. And she had plenty of help.

Eric was there every day in the summer — and when school began, every day after class. His mother even came with him sometimes to help him assist customers. She discovered that it was a fun way to get to know Eric better.

Mrs. Applebaum didn't always come to the store, however. Lots of times, Eric was there without her. And since he was part of the store's staff now, he felt very at ease showing the other children where things were and how they worked. Sometimes the children came in just

to see Eric and play with him. They especially loved it when he built his Lincoln Log masterpieces. Eric finally had something he had always, deep down, wanted very much — friends his own age.

Bellini continued to bring his beautiful books up from the basement as he always did. He was still silent and hard-working. But Mahoney was sure that, from time to time, she caught him looking around the store and smiling.

Henry stopped being an accountant. No longer content to be a counting mutant, he asked Mahoney if he could work there at the Emporium and she gladly agreed. Nothing gave him greater pleasure than helping some child find a stuffed dinosaur or showing how to best toss a paper airplane.

The person whose life changed the most, though, was Molly Mahoney. She suddenly found that she was able to finish the things she started. The pictures in her apartment all got hung. The dishes were washed. The songs she still loved to write were all finished without delay. Even Mortimer the zebra, who now lived in her apartment, found life there to be enjoyably complete.

Mr. Magorium had been right all along. Mahoney simply had to find the magic that was in her in order to live the most amazing life possible. And that was exactly the sort of life she lived.